Night Train to Lisbon

ALSO BY EMILY GRAYSON

Waterloo Station
The Fountain
The Observatory
The Gazebo

Night Train to Lisbon

Emily Grayson

wm

WILLIAM MORROW
An Imprint of HarperCollins*Publishers*

This book is a work of fiction. The characters, incidents, and dialogue are drawn from the author's imagination and are not to be construed as real. Any resemblance to actual events or persons, living or dead, is entirely coincidental.

HarperCollins books may be purchased for educational, business, or sales promotional use. For information please write: Special Markets Department, HarperCollins Publishers Inc., 10 East 53rd Street, New York, NY 10022.

FIRST EDITION

Designed by Kelly S. Too

Printed on acid-free paper

Library of Congress Cataloging-in-Publication Data

Grayson, Emily.
    Night train to Lisbon : a novel / Emily Grayson.—1st ed.
        p.   cm.
    ISBN 0-06-054264-0 (acid-free paper)
        1. Americans—Europe—Fiction.   2. World War, 1939–1945—Fiction.
3. Connecticut—Fiction.   4. Europe—Fiction.   5. Young women—Fiction.
I. Title.

PS3557.R337N54   2004
813'.54—dc22   2003068895

---

04 05 06 07 08 JTC/RRD 10 9 8 7 6 5 4 3 2 1

Acknowledgments

The author would like to thank Claire Wachtel and Jennifer Pooley for their expert editorial guidance.

Night Train to Lisbon

CHAPTER ONE

Once upon a time, her mother would begin, and Carson Weatherell to this day retained a strong memory of being a very young girl in a canopy bed curling up tighter, closer. The stories were always the same: a beautiful princess marries a handsome if fairly shallow prince, and spends her entire married life living in the same kind of splendor to which she's always been accustomed. "Someday," her mother would assure Carson when the story was over, "you will be that princess." Then she would kiss her daughter on the forehead and turn to leave the room.

The Weatherells were by far the wealthiest family in their town of Marlowe, Connecticut, a fortune made generations earlier in nautical supplies. Each generation of Weatherell men tended to the fortune as though it were a fire, stoking it worriedly and religiously, and eventually passing on to the next generation the responsibility for keeping the flame alive. And each generation of Weatherell women enjoyed spending that fortune, fashioning homes for their families that were at once comfortable and luxurious, and inevitably the envy of all the neighbors. In 1936, among the expansive homes of Marlowe with low stone walls and endless lawns, the Weatherells' was the most gracious. It would be unfair to say that Carson took her circumstances for granted; there was, after all, a depression on, and the papers were full of stories about bank runs and breadlines. Still, that outside world could seem distant indeed, if you had just turned eighteen, possessed blond hair, hazel eyes, and very pale skin, and understood that your wealth and your unambiguous beauty gave you a certain power, especially over boys.

All of which made Carson no different from any of her friends at school—or "school," for what the Miss Purslane Academy for Girls offered the haughty, daydreamy girls enrolled there tended to fall under the category of either etiquette or horsemanship. Mostly, what these girls were taught was to be just like their mothers. To the extent that any one of them had a responsibility or an ambition, it was this, and this, in Carson's view, was a perfectly fine goal to set for oneself. After all, what else was there for a princess-in-waiting to do?

In the late spring of that year, however, Philippa Weatherell received a letter from London. The return address was Claridge's Hotel, and the letter was from Philippa's younger sister, Jane. Jane had always been a bit of a renegade, running off to London to marry a man no one in the family really understood. Though Lawrence Emmett was impeccably bred, an Englishman with starched cuffs and collar who'd been to Eton and Cambridge, he had a stern and sarcastic manner that put most people off. But Jane seemed genuinely in love with him, and the couple, childless, had stayed on in London, where Lawrence now worked for the Ministry of Defence, and where they lived in a beautifully appointed suite at Claridge's.

"My dear Pippa," the letter began:

I know it's been a while since I've written, and please let me offer my apologies, for there's really no excuse. But Lawrence's work keeps us quite busy, sending us off to weekend house parties and the like. It's really a bit of a bore (how many poor little foxes can these men chase, for God's sake?), and I've been pestering good old Lawrence to take me away somewhere exciting, and FINALLY he's agreed to take me to the Continent in June: first Paris, and then Portugal, to which I haven't been in years, though I have happy memories of swimming off the coast there with Lawrence years ago, drinking local, fruity sangria, and eating those delicious fried almonds that they always used to serve. (I wonder if they still do?)

Why am I telling you all of this? you may wonder. Well, Pippa dear, I would very much like to do something special for my niece, Carson, who I have not seen since she was . . . oh, twelve or thirteen, I believe, and who has now just graduated from high school, so you tell me. As her aunt and godmother, I would like to offer her a special gift. Lawrence and I have talked it over and we wonder if Carson would care to join us in London next month, to travel first to Paris with me for a week or so, and then accompany Lawrence and me on our sojourn to Portugal. It should prove to be a delightful trip; we'll be traveling by train—first-class carriage from Paris to Lisbon—and we've already booked two sleeping compartments, one for Lawrence, and one for Carson and myself. (So you see? You CAN'T say no! We would lose our entire deposit on the second sleeping compartment!) Once in Portugal, Lawrence and I have rented a lovely, not-too-pretentious villa on the coast in Sintra, not too far from Lisbon, complete with small staff.

I think Carson will have the time of her life, and at the end of the summer we shall return her to you, bronzed and happy and ready to begin her adult life back in Connecticut. (No doubt soon to be marrying a young man you've probably already got your eye on for her, hmmmm, Pip?)

I know you will worry about Carson, as any mother would while her daughter is in new and unfamiliar circumstances, but we promise to take excellent care of her. Of course there is lots of talk about political unrest in Europe, what with the German situation and all, but Lawrence feels that, for the foreseeable future, Europe is stable (with the exception of Spain, of course), and I do trust him in these matters. Please let Carson come. It will be so much fun, not to mention the fact that, as you well know, an introduction to European ways is de rigueur for any young American lady entering society.

Your loving (and hopeful) sister,

Jane

In fact, Jane was right; Philippa did have her eye on someone for Carson, though she'd told no one her thoughts on the matter. But then, she didn't need to. It was obvious. It was *assumed*. If Carson Weatherell was a princess, then surely Harris Black would be her prince.

The Black family had moved to Connecticut from Minnesota only a few years earlier, and lived in an estate right on the water. Gordon Black owned buildings and hotels, and his wife owned shoes, plenty of them, and their son, Harris, sweet-natured and easygoing, was as good-looking a specimen as Carson. He was tall and muscled, with a cleft in his chin that seemed to have been surgically placed there, so perfect was it. He was the richest boy in town, she was the richest girl, their parents knew one another and got along, and both Carson and Harris seemed to want the same things in life, which were no different from what their parents had wanted before them. Of *course* the two of them would one day become a couple, eventually to live together ever after, perhaps even happily so. This was more than assumed; it was to be *expected*. Which was why, on the evening of the Memorial Day dance at the country club, the unofficial opening of the summer social season in Marlowe, Connecticut, Carson found herself experiencing an illicit thrill in watching Harris's response to her news—or, more accurately, in watching Harris's attempts to *conceal* his response to the fact that she would be spending the summer abroad.

"Really?" he said, when Carson's mother slipped this bit of information into the conversation as if she were merely making an observation about the evening's fashions, which was in fact what she had been doing—she and Miranda Black both. Harris had been twisted halfway around in his chair, drumming his fingers on the white linen tablecloth in time with the orchestra, distractedly appraising the couples on the dance floor. Now he looked from Carson to Philippa and back again to Carson. "Is that wise?" Harris said. "There's talk of war, after all."

It was his mother who answered him, dismissing the thought with a wave of the paper fan she'd been using to cool herself. "There's always talk of war," Miranda Black said. "It's what men talk *about*. If women waited for talk of war to subside, we should never travel abroad."

5

The four of them—Harris and Carson and their mothers—were sitting at a table decorated with a red, white, and blue bunting Liberty Bell centerpiece. Mr. Black and Mr. Weatherell had removed themselves to the other side of the dance floor, where they stood among a group of men at the bar, discussing business perhaps, or—as Miranda Black suggested—war.

"I'm sure you're right, Mother," Harris said. "But anyone who's seen the latest news from Germany—"

"Since when have you taken such an interest in world affairs?" his mother interrupted, giving her son a curious smile. "I don't believe I've ever seen you reading anything but the sporting news."

"I merely thought—" Harris began. He looked down at his lime rickey, gave the glass a couple of twirls, then glanced back up at Carson. "What I mean to say is, I suppose I'd assumed that Carson would be *here* this summer."

He turned slightly red, as if he hadn't meant to place quite so much emphasis on the *here* of the matter. Harris would be going off to college in the fall—Yale, like his father before him, and his father's father before that. So it only would have made sense if he was planning to spend the summer before college at home, attempting to win the attentions of the elegant and aloof Carson Weatherell. It had made sense to Carson, anyway, when she'd thought about her summer, and now she saw that it had made sense to Harris, too. And to be honest, she couldn't say that his slightly flustered response to the news of her change in plans displeased her.

"Well," Harris's mother said, "Carson *won't* be here, she'll be *there*, and she will be the better woman for it." Miranda

Black was fair-haired and overweight, and she had no trouble speaking with authority. "You know," she went on, fixing her son with a cautioning look, "this is a splendid opportunity for Carson. It will expand her horizons. She'll learn how to be a proper hostess. She'll learn how to dress. She'll learn to tell a Vermeer from a Veronese. And one day she will be a better wife for having taken the so-called grand tour, just as Philippa and I did in our day, isn't that right, Philippa dear?" she added, turning to Carson's mother.

But before Philippa could answer, Harris cut in.

"Well, why don't we hear from Carson herself?" he said. "Everyone seems to know what's best for her. Maybe she has an opinion on the subject of her own future?"

His mother drew back slightly in her chair, as if summoning her resources for a response, but before she had a chance to say anything, Philippa spoke.

"Nonsense," she said. "Your mother is right, Harris. This trip is just what Carson needs. It's the best thing that could have happened to her. It's her chance to go and see the world before she comes back here and settles down for good. Isn't that right, Carson dear?" she said, and then she reached out and closed a hand over her daughter's, pressing it into the white tablecloth hard enough to make an impression in the soft fabric, as if sealing some sort of unspoken pact.

One week later, Carson set sail for London on the *Queen Mary*. She brought so much luggage with her that to the uninitiated it might have appeared as though she were planning on moving permanently to the continent of Europe. But she was only doing as her mother advised: if you're going to go abroad, do it in style. There was a bon voyage party in Carson's stateroom while the ship was docked in New York; her parents were there, as were their friends the Blacks, as was champagne. There were pops and whoops. There were shouts and laughter. There were toasts to Carson's health, to her good fortune, to upcoming adventures. And there was, in the end, an awkward moment when the parents said farewell and hugged her good-bye and withdrew from the cabin, and Harris lingered behind. He raised his champagne flute to Carson, as if to propose a toast, but he said nothing. Instead, he took one last gulp, placed his glass on the table next to the champagne bucket, and said, "Well, I imagine I'll see you when you return."

"You mean *if* I return," Carson said.

She regretted it immediately. She didn't know why she'd said it. Maybe because nobody was listening—nobody but Harris, and he didn't really count, since they were the same age and had never needed to worry about keeping up appearances around each other. Anyway, Carson hadn't meant anything by it; of course she would be returning. Where else did she have to go? It was a joke, a gesture, part of the Carson Weatherell come-hither armor, and she supposed she had expected Harris to return the jest in kind: *Oh, yes, I'm sure you'll find everything you've ever wanted in some little village in the provinces of Portugal. And who knows? Perhaps you'll even meet a mysterious stranger.* Instead, his face had clouded briefly, at least before he had a chance to recover. But then he did recover, and Carson reassured herself that she hadn't wounded him, not in the least. Harris raised his chin and smiled, and he gave her a friendly if appropriately hesitant peck on the cheek, and then he stepped outside the stateroom to leave Carson alone on her maiden voyage.

Not entirely alone, of course. That would have been unseemly for a single young woman of her station. A chaperone had been sent with her for the crossing, a little woman named Mrs. Adele, who had worked for the family in one capacity or another for many years, and who would return to Connecticut once she'd safely delivered Carson to Claridge's. But Mrs. Adele's dour presence hardly counted as companionship, and when Carson confessed that she really wasn't much of a conversationalist and would prefer to keep to herself except at meals, the relief seemed mutual. So Carson did just that for much of the crossing: she kept to herself. Often she stayed in her stateroom to sip flat champagne and read one of the romance novels she'd brought with her (the current one, by a Mrs. Lucille Lovett Davies, was called *Alice of the Springtime*, and was about a young woman of simple circumstance who falls in love with a Scottish laird). Other times, Carson sat by the rail and looked out at the green-black ocean, thinking how far she was from home, and how far she was from her destination, and wondering why, after all, she was going to Europe in the first place. She knew it was "the thing to do." Some of her friends from school were making similar trips that summer, and everyone had seemed so excited by the prospect of going abroad, talking about the clothing they were going to buy and the landmarks they were going to visit and, yes, the mysterious strangers they were going to meet.

Everyone but Carson.

Oh, she had *seemed* excited, all right. She'd gone along with the gushing and the well-wishing and the hushed disclosures of what one really hoped to discover on such a journey. But the fact was, Carson hadn't been sure she should go. Everyone else, though, had seemed so sure for her—everyone except Harris, of course—that Carson had found herself simply sailing along with the prevailing sentiment, because, well, that's what one did.

Now, though, alone on board this vast ship full of thousands of people, staring past page 103 of *Alice of the Springtime* toward the porthole that revealed the same waves she had seen the day before, and the day before that, she wondered what it was she was hoping to find in Europe. Certainly, based on everything she'd heard or read or seen, she found the idea of Europe exciting in some ill-defined way. Yet she felt a kind of anxiety welling up like a crisis within her, and she recognized it as something she couldn't blame on the rolling of the ocean. It was a feeling of tentativeness that she'd often identified in herself—a tentativeness that anyone who knew her would have been surprised to learn about. It came precisely from having been assigned no responsibilities or ambitions— or so Carson had always told herself. But hadn't all the girls she knew from Miss Purslane's been assigned no responsibilities or ambitions, other than to model themselves after their mothers? Yet *they* suffered no tentativeness. On the contrary. That single responsibility, that sole goal, had quite sufficed. Those girls were just as headstrong and as certain as Harris Black's mother, and they sailed straight for Europe as if it was their destiny, as if it was their due. So what was it about Carson? Alone on the ship for days at a time, she had no choice but to ask herself what she was afraid of. The threat of war? That was real, but as Amanda Black had said, no more real than it ever was. The food? The weather? The travel? The people?

All of these. All of them and none of them at the same time.

On the fourth day of the voyage, Carson began to grasp what it was. She had settled herself in her usual spot, near the rear of the *Queen Mary*—the aft, as she now knew to call it. Leaning back in her deck chair, wrapping herself in a thin wool blanket, she stared out at the ship's wake, that whitish-green churning turbulence billowing backward as far as she could see, narrowing away from the full width of the ship all the way to the infinite nothingness of the horizon. Somewhere out there was home. But not *just* home. It wasn't just Marlowe where she longed to be at that moment—had longed to be ever since she felt the first unmistakable jarring in her legs that signaled the ship's slippage from the mainland. It wasn't just the Weatherell estate where she wanted to be. It wasn't even in her own bed. It was in her own bed *as a young girl again.*

Carson closed her eyes. She wrapped herself tighter. She could see it now, hear it now: her mother telling her that story about the princess and the prince. That was where she longed to be. That was who she longed to be: someone whose future was certain, was unchangeable; whose future held no *chance* of change, no surprises, no knowledge of a still-distant but nonetheless ever-nearing continent looming larger at her back, with its cities and buildings, its cathedrals and catacombs, its clink of unfamiliar coins, its Babel-like chatter, and— Carson now understood—its endless array of possibilities.

Aunt Jane and Uncle Lawrence had festooned their suite at Claridge's with ribbons and a banner declaring WELCOME,

CARSON, and they had even sent for a tray of small, carefully constructed hors d'oeuvres and yet another silver bucket of champagne on ice. They seemed very pleased with themselves, and Carson made an appropriate effort to seem in turn very pleased with them.

"Oh," she said, "this is so elaborate. You're treating me as though I'm visiting royalty or something."

"Believe me," Aunt Jane replied, taking her by the elbow, "your visit is far more interesting than the one we had recently from a deadly dull Greek prince and his entourage."

"A prince?" Carson heard herself say. She hadn't meant to blurt this out, to risk seeming so uncouth. She realized as soon as she said it that her aunt was probably kidding. Aunt Jane had a certain bright, impish spirit about her, a playful manner that Carson wasn't used to—not, at any rate, from her mother, who was, after all, Jane's sister. But a prince, it turned out, was precisely what Aunt Jane meant.

"Oh yes," said Uncle Lawrence. "Since I've been with the government—even in my rather low position, mind you— we've gotten to know quite a few dignitaries."

"Lawrie, your position isn't low," said Aunt Jane. "It's perfectly important."

"Yes, yes, Janie, I'm chief bottle washer and paper filer, is that it?" Lawrence said with a slight smile, and again Carson wasn't sure whether or not he was teasing. In truth, she knew little of substance about her aunt and uncle.

"Stick with *us*, Carson," said Aunt Jane, "and over the summer you'll meet all sorts of people."

"Quite right. All the wrong sorts," said Uncle Lawrence, and his wife pushed him gently.

"Now, don't say that, Lawrie," said Aunt Jane. "You'll scare the girl off. Now, let me get a good look at you, Carson. I haven't seen you in so long. Too long."

And with that, Aunt Jane reached out and took Carson's hands in her own. Carson felt herself smile shyly, and then she looked back at her aunt and uncle. They hadn't seen her in six years, since a brief swing through Connecticut during some diplomatic trip that had brought Uncle Lawrence to New York City. All that Carson remembered of that meeting was wondering, as she entered the library where her parents and aunt and uncle had gathered for the cocktail hour, whether she should curtsy; these guests were from England, after all. Carson felt herself smiling now at the memory. Back then, she imagined, she must have seemed an awkward girl, tall and thin and, probably, a little dull, at least from the perspective of a worldly couple such as her aunt and uncle.

"You've changed, no surprise," her aunt announced now. "You're all grown up."

"I should say so," Uncle Lawrence echoed. "She's eighteen, Jane, an age at which, if I remember the recesses of my own distant past correctly, nobody wants an aunt hanging on to their limbs for too long."

"Oh, you," Aunt Jane said to her husband, but she let go of Carson's hands.

Carson couldn't help herself. She smiled shyly again at all this attention. She, of course, had no idea how much *they'd* changed in the past six years. It wasn't in the nature of a typically self-involved twelve-year-old to give a visiting aunt and uncle much thought. Now, though, Carson returned their

steady, studying gaze, and realized that she was seeing them—
really seeing them—for the first time.

They were a smart-looking couple in their midthirties.
Jane was tall and lively, her husband pale and balding, but
made more attractive by his wry smile. Carson knew that her
mother didn't really like Uncle Lawrence very much, but for
some reason, she herself did. *He's fun,* she thought to herself.
She'd never known that. Or, perhaps, she'd never been *allowed* to know that.

"So tell us, Carson," said Uncle Lawrence, indicating that
Carson should sit on the chair opposite the couch, "what you
expect to get out of this trip of ours."

"Oh, well, you know," Carson began vaguely, and then she
parroted back the words that her mother and father had used
when they were encouraging her to accept the offer, and that
she'd heard her friends use when they'd talked about their
own opportunities to go abroad. "It will give me a real education, the kind I've never had before. It will teach me a few
things about how people live in other parts of the world—"

"Oh, enough," Uncle Lawrence cut in brusquely. "Don't
tell us what you think we want to hear. Tell us what you really
think."

"What I really think?"

"Yes," encouraged Aunt Jane. "Go on."

What she really thought. Carson wasn't quite sure how to
comply with this request. It surely wasn't one she was used to
fielding. But she was tired. She'd been on a ship for days, and
then when she'd gotten off the ship, she felt as if she were still
on the ship, and in all honesty the train ride from the docks
in Southampton to London had done nothing to dispel the

notion that she hadn't quite landed on solid ground, what with the rhythmic rocking of the railway carriage, and then there was the time difference between London and Connecticut, so that even though it had crept up on her gradually on board the *Queen Mary*, she couldn't quite shake the conviction that five in the afternoon, when she joined her aunt and uncle in their drawing room for the kinds of drinks that got served in glass decanters and usually signaled a tipping over into the evening hours, was nonetheless noon at home—well, when the request came for her to say what she really thought, Carson actually did.

"I've kind of been dreading the whole thing."

She raised a hand to her mouth. Her uncle's laughter, however, offered her all the reassurance she needed. Then her aunt's as well. And not just reassurance. Encouragement.

"No offense, please," she began.

"None taken!" her uncle said.

"But I'm really not one for travel," Carson went on. "Oh, I know Europe is supposed to be splendid and all, and that in fact it's an exciting place—for some good reasons and some less-than-good reasons—but I just wanted to stay home this summer and lie around a lot and read, and see my friends, that sort of thing, same as I've always done."

"I see," said Aunt Jane, wiping a tear. "You wanted to loaf, and we're making you soak up culture. Is that it?"

"Something like it," admitted Carson. She was tearing up now, too, though not from laughter. She hadn't been laughing at all, in fact. Her uncle and aunt, she supposed, had found her confusion comical, and Carson herself could appreciate the comic potential of a time-lagged niece blurting out to an aunt and uncle the unholy truth regarding her visit to the Continent. And maybe she was indeed loopy from lack of sleep. But what touched her now, she realized, what really moved her, was the opportunity she'd been given to reveal the feelings she'd been holding inside, and the release that accompanied her finally doing so.

"I promise," said Aunt Jane, "that there won't be too much soaking up. You're not a sponge, you're a young woman."

"And a good-looking one," said Uncle Lawrence. "There will be men here in Europe who will want to get to know you, Carson, even if you don't particularly want to get to know them. They can be quite forward, you know. It's another thing that the Continent is famous for, even more than its food and its paintings."

Men. Carson was taken aback by the reference. Yes, her friends had mentioned men when they talked about going abroad this summer, but that, Carson knew, was just so much girl talk—girls talking about boys but straining to sound grown up and sophisticated. *Boys,* Carson and her friends knew well how to handle. They'd been doing so for years: receiving the quiet flirtations of a Harris Black, rebuffing them, and receiving still more flirtatious advances in turn. It was a game, one for which she and her friends all understood the rules.

But in Europe? What game of flirtation was played here? Her uncle was right. The men here seemed much more reckless, dressed differently, were more experienced. They called out to women on the street, they whistled, they signaled with their hands. They played a different game, and they played by different rules.

"You don't have to worry," Carson assured her uncle. "I'm not going to pay any attention to the men here."

"Good," he said. "It's one less thing for us to concern ourselves with."

"Yes," she said, "one less thing"—as if she were counting down the duties she would have to perform before being allowed to return home.

Over the following week, Carson fulfilled some of those duties. On a whirlwind tour of London, she was taken by her aunt to the Tower of London, Hyde Park, Westminster Abbey. She was then ferried across the English Channel to Paris, where the two women shared a room at the Ritz, shopped in intimate, luxurious boutiques, strolled along the Champs Élysées, outfitted themselves in Chanel suits and wide picture hats, and every evening ate meals that relied heavily on goose fat and truffles.

It was at one of these meals that Carson ate something that would sicken her hours later. She was never exactly sure what it had been: an escargot baked in garlicky butter, maybe, or an oyster sitting cool and gelatinous inside the saucer of its elaborate shell. In the middle of the night, Carson bolted from her bed and went into the marble bathroom she shared with her aunt. She spent the rest of the night in that bathroom, alternately sitting and lying on the cold floor. Her aunt did all she could, stroking Carson's hair, having ice delivered to the room and feeding her niece crushed chips of it, but Carson was desperately ill with the kind of food poisoning that is unrelenting until it has completely run its course.

That course ended around daybreak. Carson, weak as a rag

doll, went back to bed and pulled the blankets around herself. Apparently, she thought, this trip to Europe had been too much for her after all. A doctor was called in, an imperious Frenchman with spectacles and a pointed beard, who took her pulse and peered down her throat, as if searching for the offending morsel of food, and then shrugged, saying something in an incomprehensible torrent of French, and departed. The next day, when finally she was strong enough to sit up in bed and sip a cup of beef tea that had been ordered from room service, Carson announced to her aunt, "I hope you and Uncle Lawrence won't mind very much if I call it a day."

" 'Call it a day'? And what exactly does that mean?" her aunt asked.

"It means that I think I want to go home," said Carson. "I've seen London and Paris. And I've seen a great deal of the inside of a Parisian toilet bowl. I think it's pretty much enough for one summer."

"But what about Portugal?" said Aunt Jane with rising protest. "We've booked the train. *And* rented the house. We've got the entire summer there, Carson. Did you forget about that?"

"No," said Carson. "But I just don't want to go. I want to go home." In an even weaker voice, she added, "You've always asked for my honest response. Well, there it is."

Her aunt stared at her with both pity and, Carson thought, some degree of contempt.

"For God's sake," Aunt Jane said quietly. "I thought you were going to be different."

"Excuse me?"

"Oh, nothing," said her aunt.

"Please. Tell me," said Carson.

Aunt Jane sighed and turned away, as if considering carefully how to phrase what she wanted to say. She walked over to the window and pushed aside the drapes, then let them drop together again.

"Your mother and I—we were always very different," she finally said. "Philippa stayed close to home, and I went off exploring. I guess I've always had a fantasy that you would take after me instead of your own mother." Her aunt turned back to her. "Well, I suppose that was just my fantasy, wasn't it? The niece off in the States who was the spitting image of her aunt. The niece who longed for adventure, just like her aunt once did."

Though she still felt weak and drained, Carson had enough energy left in her to take umbrage. "I could be like that," she said, "if I wanted."

"Well, then *show* it," Aunt Jane said, crossing back to the foot of the bed. "Sure, it's fine to live a life like your mother does, staying in Connecticut and marrying the 'right' sort of man. I'm not saying there's anything wrong with that, Carson."

"Yes, you are," Carson found herself replying. "You are, Aunt Jane." She paused, shocked to hear herself standing up to her aunt. "I know my mother hasn't been very bold in her life. But she's happy, she really is. Some people want a life that's already laid out for them."

Her aunt regarded Carson across the length of the bed.

"Yes, that's certainly true," Aunt Jane finally said softly. She came and sat down beside her niece on the blanket, taking

Carson's hand in hers. "Which sort of person are you?" she asked. "Are you the kind who wants things to be a certain, safe way? Or are you the other kind?"

Carson, of course, knew the answer. She'd known it since that afternoon on the ship when she'd sat in the deck chair and stared out at the horizon and sorted out her feelings. But now she was sitting in a different place, with a different view. She looked about the room, at its long gold drapes through which she could just make out the warm light of a Paris afternoon. Those drapes, that window, was another kind of horizon, wasn't it? What lay beyond it? Carson could catch the sounds of people shouting in French, of horns honking, of horses' hooves clopping, of life being lived as surely as it was lived on the far quieter streets of Marlowe, Connecticut. And beyond Paris lay the rest of Europe—for Carson, the Continent remained undiscovered, unexplored, unknown.

What sort of person *was* she? She thought she'd known for sure, back on the ship. But maybe what she thought she'd known for sure was only what she'd always been told about herself. Maybe if she'd always been told something else— maybe if she'd been raised by her aunt instead of her mother—she'd be just as sure she was someone else, someone for whom change and possibilities and adventure were nectar, not poison.

Who was she? Suddenly she understood that all an eighteen-year-old girl in her position could possibly know for certain was that there was no way to know yet. If she was indeed like her mother, there would be no shame in that. In learning this about herself, she would end up going back to Connecticut at the end of summer, ready to return to a life she understood. But if, somehow, she was *different*, then this, too, she would learn. And at the end of the summer she would return to Connecticut with this knowledge, facing a life that would hold . . . who knew what?

Carson Weatherell was tired and wrung out and confused. She was irritable from food poisoning and from being away from home, but she understood now that to turn her back on everything she was being offered would be not only selfish and insulting to her aunt and uncle, but also hurtful to herself.

She had to know who she was. Maybe she wouldn't find out here in Europe, but then again maybe she would. The prospect of an overnight train ride to Portugal was nerve-racking, not to mention uncomfortable sounding, but the thought of turning it down, after coming this far, was unforgivable.

"All right," Carson said, gently pulling back the blanket beneath which she lay. "I'm in."

CHAPTER TWO

The atmosphere inside an overnight train is very much its own world. As soon as you board and find your own compartment, you have entered a place unlike the one you have just left. Narrower, dimmer, and more dramatic: these are the qualities of train life, in which everything is compressed, and the rest of the world simply passes you by in a glassy blur of green and brown and gold.

This was what Carson noticed as she and her aunt arranged themselves inside their sleeping compartment in the Gare St. Lazare, on board the train that would soon be leaving for Lisbon. Uncle Lawrence had just arrived from London and met his wife and niece at the station, and was now settling into his adjoining compartment. He was in a snappish mood, Carson noted, for he barely said hello and he muttered as he handed the porter his bags and briefcase, which was fairly bulging with work.

"Darling, you're not planning on working during the ride, are you?" Aunt Jane asked.

"I'm afraid I have to," Uncle Lawrence replied. "There's nothing to be done about it. Whitehall has its needs, you know, which tend to override the needs of civil servants like me."

Aunt Jane told Carson she was determined to let neither Uncle Lawrence's distractedness nor Carson's own reluctance to travel ruin the trip. "We're simply going to have fun," said Jane, "and that's all there is to it."

And Carson had to admit that there was something sort of grand and wonderful and nineteenth century about train travel. European trains were so different from trains in the States. Here, the first-class carriages seemed like old-fashioned coaches, their interiors decorated with inlaid wood and plush, faded maroon velvet and brass trim. The compartment meant for Carson and her aunt was surprisingly spacious, though the steamer trunk that the women were taking to Portugal took up a good deal of the space, even when stood on end. There were curtains sashed on the window, and a basket of fruit sitting on its wide ledge. A sliding glass door kept the women separate from the rest of the train, though every time someone passed by, Carson couldn't help but strain to catch a glimpse.

The other passengers on the Paris–Lisbon train spoke a variety of languages: French, Portuguese, Spanish, Italian, English, all of which came together as if in one mostly incomprehensible cloud above Carson's head. There were ladies dressed in chic tailored outfits and others in old-fashioned, heavy muslin mantillas; there were gentlemen in suits and some more casually attired. Children clattered loudly up and down the corridor, followed inevitably a moment later by nannies or mothers crying "*Pierre, arrête-toi!*" Or "Stop this moment, Edmund!"

Carson was still feeling somewhat weak from her bout of food poisoning in Paris, but something about the peculiar and

peculiarly festive life inside this train was making her feel better rather quickly. In fact, when Aunt Jane asked if Carson
wanted to rest before dinner, she shook her head.

"Can we go exploring instead?" she asked.

Her aunt looked at her with an expression that suggested
she was trying to hide her surprise. "Of course, dear," she said.
"I'd like nothing better."

The two women headed out of the sleeping compartment
into the corridor. Next door, in his solitary sleeper, they could
see Uncle Lawrence through his door, his head bent studiously over a sheaf of papers.

Aunt Jane sighed. "Carson," she said over her shoulder as
they made their way down the corridor, "when you meet a
wonderful man someday, years from now, and fall in love, I
only hope he doesn't have a mistress, like your uncle does."

"Pardon?" said Carson.

But Aunt Jane only smiled. "I mean that your uncle's mistress is his *work*," she said. "Sometimes, I can get extremely
jealous of those endless sheets of paper he pores over." She
shrugged. "Oh, well," she continued. "I'm so glad I've got you
here on this journey to keep me company. We women need to
stick together."

As she threaded her way along the first-class corridor, Carson couldn't help peering into the other compartments. It was
like racing through an art gallery at closing time, she thought;
each glimpse through a glass door afforded a different combination of poses, of reading or talking or simply staring out at
the countryside, but the theme of the various tableaux was
the same: first-class passengers in quiet repose. Only at the
very end of the car did she find a compartment with an at-

mosphere that seemed markedly different from the others'. All the passengers in here were young men in shirtsleeves, and they were playing cards, which were spread out on someone's upturned trunk, and they were drinking bottles of pop and smoking and talking in an animated fashion. Carson couldn't help herself. She paused, as if she needed a moment to fully absorb a scene where so much was happening at once, and all of it behind a scrim of smoke—as if it really were a scene being presented for her close consideration. The men were so intent on their cards, so serious, yet they were so obviously enjoying themselves, too, with their fast-moving mouths forming words she couldn't hear. And then one of the men looked up from his fan of cards. He was wearing a white cotton shirt and loosely knotted tie, and he had dark brown hair and a crooked smile. Carson knew these details to be true, because when he looked up, he looked at her, and she looked back, forgetting for the moment that this wasn't at all a scene being presented for her consideration but lives being actually lived by people who could see her, and seeing her, smile, as this young man did now. Carson caught herself then. She raised a hand to her lips in embarrassment and turned away and quickly hurried on, pushing through the heavy doors that separated the cars.

"What was keeping you?" Aunt Jane asked, waiting in the aisle of the next car, but Carson said nothing. She didn't know why she had stared at that man. No, she did know. It wasn't simply that the scene she'd witnessed was so lively, or that she'd lost herself in the seeming illusion of the moment. It was the man himself. He wasn't conventionally handsome, yet she had wanted to keep looking at him—had found herself staring at him for that very reason. His features weren't predictable. They weren't classic—weren't symmetrical. They were . . . individual, and somehow more interesting for that. This was an idea of "good-looking" that was new to Carson, she realized, one that she'd never before considered. As she and Aunt Jane strode through the train, peeking in at the dining car, which even now was being laid with linen and silver and glassware by a fleet of efficient-looking Frenchmen in white jackets, Carson felt a light-headedness, and knew that it had nothing to do with the illness from which she was recovering.

Was it really coincidence, later, that brought Carson Weatherell elbow to elbow with the man she'd stared at? For that night at dinner, when he was seated beside her in the dining car, she felt an excitement, a prickle of fear and curiosity that seemed to run lightly down the back of her neck.

Carson and her aunt and uncle were having dinner at a four-person table set for four, when the waiter appeared and apologetically began asking in stilted English if they would mind terribly if "a lone diner, a gentleman he seem very nice," sat with them this evening. "His friends they come earlier to dinner and he did not join them," the waiter explained. "So now he is . . . *tout seul,* and seeing how you are a table of four . . ."

"*Bien sûr,*" said Aunt Jane. "Why not?"

Uncle Lawrence simply rolled his eyes. Carson herself had no opinion on the matter until the lanky young man in the tweed jacket approached the table and Carson realized who he was.

"Sit down, sit down," said Aunt Jane. "We've barely begun our soup. Please join us."

"I'm terribly sorry," said the young man. His accent was English, educated, though with a subtle hint of something less fine beneath it. "You see, my friends and I, we were playing whist earlier, and I gather that I fell asleep shortly after the game. They came to the early seating, and they didn't want to wake me, and so I find myself in need of food."

"It's perfectly fine," said Uncle Lawrence as though he were already bored with the explanation and simply wanted to get on with the meal. Then Lawrence picked up his soup spoon and dipped it into the shallow bowl of consommé.

"I'm Alec Breve," the young man said to no one in particular. "I promise not to put my elbows on the table or try to eat my peas with a knife."

Carson regarded him from her seat at his side. He had a wry smile on his face: crooked again, she noticed. Throughout the remainder of the meal, Alec Breve carried on an animated conversation with Jane and Lawrence. They talked about the situation in Spain, and in Germany, and occasionally Carson put in a few words, but for the most part she felt like someone with almost nothing to say. Everyone else at this table was full of life experience and stories about themselves and their escapades in the world. Alec Breve, she quickly learned, was a physicist at Cambridge University who, with his group of friends, was traveling to an international science conference, where he was going to deliver his first formal paper before an audience.

"I'm quite nervous, actually," he admitted. "The last time I remember speaking in public was during a school-days performance of *Hamlet*."

"Ah," said Aunt Jane. "Did you play the prince himself?"

Alec Breve smiled. "Not quite," he said. "But the other fellows tell me I made a simply lovely Ophelia." He shrugged. "That's what happens when you attend an all-boys school, as most boys in England do. You're forced into Shakespearean roles that tend to, well, strain credulity."

"Just like back when Shakespeare wrote them," put in Carson.

"Yes, that's right," said Alec. "No women were allowed on-stage in Elizabethan England. Though I daresay, nowadays, there are some wonderful actresses portraying these roles. Even in Portugal this summer, you know, you will be able to catch a Shakespeare play."

"Is that so?" said Uncle Lawrence.

"When I received the literature for my scientific conference," Alec said, "I was also sent some information about local events and so forth. Seems that a Portuguese troupe will be performing *Romeo and Juliet* sometime next week. If you'll be in the area, perhaps you might like to attend."

"I don't speak Portuguese," Carson said.

"Doesn't matter," said Alec. "I think you can still get the gist of it. It's a love story. That's a fairly international theme."

"As a scientist," said Uncle Lawrence suddenly, lowering his glass of claret, "surely you don't find yourself entertaining too many questions in your work about the nature of love."

"Perhaps not," said Alec. "Though I wish I did. My work tends to be far duller than all that."

"What *is* the nature of your work?" Uncle Lawrence asked.

"Oh, it will only bore you," said Alec.

"Try me," Lawrence persisted, and Carson realized she'd

never seen her uncle quite so engaged with another person, quite so lively and invested in the conversation. She listened, now, as Alec Breve spoke, noticing how modest he was, how embarrassed he seemed by being the center of attention.

"I'm involved in the study of thermodynamics. I conduct experiments and spend hours recording my findings into a little green notebook. Extremely dull. In fact, simply hearing an *explanation* of the nature of my work has been known to put people to sleep. I've been frequently hired by frantic mothers to come babysit their cranky youngsters. I'm told to sit near the cot and simply talk about what it is I do for a living. Within minutes—often, seconds—the child is out cold."

Everyone laughed at the joke, as well as at Alec's perfect, deadpan delivery. As dinner came to a close, Carson realized she was disappointed it was ending. Soon Alec would retreat to his compartment with his friends, probably for card games and cigars. But now, as if he was reading her thoughts, he turned to Uncle Lawrence and lightly said, "I wonder, actually, if I might borrow your niece for a little while this evening. That is, if she's willing."

Uncle Lawrence blinked slowly, like someone coming to the surface from a deep thought. "It's entirely up to Carson, I suppose," he said. "What is it you wish to borrow her for?"

"The other fellows and I are going to play a bit more cards, and one of our party has vowed that he must stay in his berth and work, if you can believe it. Work! On a train trip to Portugal! Who ever heard of such a thing?"

"Shocking," Aunt Jane said, and Carson saw her cast Uncle Lawrence a weary glance, which he in turn acknowledged with a weary sigh.

"So you see," Alec went on, "we'll need a fourth hand."

"I'm sorry, but I don't play," Carson said quietly.

Alec looked at her neutrally. "Want to learn?" he asked, and his voice was casual, as if he didn't want to put any pressure on her to say yes; as if, she realized, he didn't even really care all that much whether she said yes.

Carson looked from her uncle to her aunt, but they, too, seemed neutral. *If my mother was here,* Carson thought, *she would be giving me eye signals that told me what it was I should be doing, whether I ought to be saying yes or no.* For one of the first times in her life, Carson realized, she was being asked to make an independent decision.

"All right," said Carson, and Alec smiled.

"Good," he said. "It will make the game so much more interesting."

The atmosphere inside the compartment where the young scientists were playing cards was basically composed of smoke. Alec led her past the steamer-trunk playing surface and into a seat by the window. "Gentlemen," he said. "We have a new player among us. This is Miss Carson Weatherell, and I have a feeling she's going to be a crack whist player."

Through the gray plumes, Carson could make out the faces of three other young men. "Hello," said one, extending a hand. "Michael Morling."

"Thomas Brandon."

"Frederick Hunt," said the third. "But everyone who knows me calls me Freddy sooner or later."

"Pleased to meet you," said Carson.

"Hey, what do you know, the lady's a Yank," said Freddy

Hunt. He was a redhead with bright eyes, an impish-looking man, small and compact, who seemed like he'd be a great deal of fun as a traveling companion. Though Michael and Thomas looked the part of young scientists, Carson thought, Freddy was more like the younger brother of a scientist—a little too playful, actually, to possess a serious scientific mind.

Carson had never been called a Yank before. She was in the minority here, both as a female and as an American, and the attention was pleasurable, she realized. The game got under way, with all the men piping in to teach her the rules of play. Carson was a poor player in the beginning, but quickly caught on, and eventually she found herself winning the hand.

"What did I say?" said Alec proudly. "Didn't I tell you she'd be good?"

The men chimed in with admiration or mock anger. There were jokes and laughter, and even a few sentimental old school songs, including one that Freddy, in particular, sang with gusto and irony at the top of his lungs, while his friends egged him on:

"Oh, I miss my old college, and all of my chums . . .
The food there was dreadful, and never beat my mum's.
But the friends that I made there will be friends for my life . . .
Cherished as much as mother, and children and wife . . ."

"Oh, Freddy," said Thomas, "you make me want to cry."

"Yes, we're all going to weep into our ale," added Michael. "We're going to have *paroxysms* of sorrow."

Alec rolled his eyes and turned to Carson to explain.

"You'll have to forgive them," he said. "You see, we've all known one another since we were first-years at Cambridge, all of us studying physics. Now, each of us thought we were simply brilliant, having been told that when we were schoolboys. But upon arriving at Cambridge, we received the shock of our lives to learn that there were actually *other* men out there who were possibly as brilliant as we were— maybe even more so. Believe me, Carson, it was a comeup- pance. And the most galling fact of it all was that this . . . this"—he gestured toward Freddy—"this *infant,* who looked like someone's younger tagalong brother, was, in fact, the most brilliant one among us. He'd come out of nowhere. A Yorkshire lad. No pedigree whatsoever, and he was at Cam- bridge on a full scholarship. Saved from a life spent in the coal mines, having been rescued by a kindly geology tutor visiting Yorkshire on an expedition who happened upon the lad with the thick accent and the head full of astonishing ideas. Soon Freddy was a first-year along with the rest of us, and fairly soon afterward, the four of us were rooming to- gether at college."

"It was an extraordinary time," said Michael wistfully. "We stayed up as late as we could, just talking, playing cards—"

"Drinking," put in Freddy.

"Yes, drinking," said Michael, "but also figuring things out. Scientific problems, that sort of thing. Ever since then, we've been a sort of team. An unofficial think tank, if you will. And all of us have been given posts at dear old Cambridge, and we've got a big, rambling bachelor's flat in town, away from college life, where we can drink and carouse to our hearts' content and not be bad influences on the young."

"Except during tutorials," said Thomas. "At which point we can't help but be a terrible influence."

Carson looked from one to the other during this conversation. They were so vibrant, these men, so full of intelligence and playfulness. She scarcely knew which one of them she liked best. Well, no, that wasn't quite true. She liked Alec best, for in addition to being playful, he was handsome and considerate and genuinely interested in what she had to say. But there was something about the energy of the entire group that was exciting to be around. *Compare this*, she thought, maybe a little meanly, *with life back in Connecticut.*

The thought of Connecticut reminded Carson of money, and the subject of money reminded her that Alec had almost none of it himself. True, he and his friends were traveling first-class, but Alec had made it clear during dinner that Cambridge was footing the bill for their train travel and their accommodations once they arrived in Portugal. He himself came from modest circumstances; his father had died long ago, and his mother, who had died last year, had been a "charwoman," a term that was new to Carson but which, he quickly explained when met with her puzzled expression, meant she had cleaned other people's houses.

But it was strange, Carson realized, the way Alec didn't seem to care very much about money. Again, Connecticut came to mind. How much everyone Carson knew in Connecticut cared about money. How much *she* cared.

Or, actually, how much she *didn't* care. How much she didn't think about it, didn't *need* to think about it, except to assume that it would be there to furnish an entire life for those like herself who were lucky enough to have it. Having money was a given for someone in Carson's world. The money was always flowing, as if from some invisible underground well. In the fairy tales that her mother told before bed, in which the princess married the prince, money was naturally assumed to be present, and in her own idle thoughts about falling in love one day, it never occurred to Carson that money wouldn't be part of the equation. Never, not even once.

But here, in this smoky sleeper car, Carson found herself among men whose lives were not in any way devoted to the pursuit of money. Maybe it was the smoke, or an aftereffect of the food poisoning, or the sudden feeling of dislocation, as though she were a million miles away from the values and concerns of her Connecticut world, but Carson suddenly needed air and needed it now. She closed her eyes, and when she opened them, as though summoned by her thoughts, Alec was standing above her.

"You know, I think I need some air," he said. "Want to come?"

Carson nodded and stood, and Alec slid the compartment door open.

"This way," he said, and he led her down the aisle. They passed nighttime compartments in which porters were turning down berths, getting them ready for sleep, tucking white sheets into the red crushed velvet. Little lights were on inside the compartments, casting soft yellow glows like fireflies, while through the train windows the night sky rushed by in a blur, that French sky that would imperceptibly become a Spanish one, and then eventually a Portuguese one.

There were families inside compartments getting ready for

the night, and Carson took notice of mothers with daughters, the little well-dressed girls of first class clutching their beloved dolls tightly. She recalled her own beloved doll when she was a girl, a flaxen-haired, blue-eyed rag doll named Emmeline. What had become of her? She was probably put away into a box somewhere, forgotten, the way all childhood treasures eventually are. And now, as Alec led Carson down the aisle, she went past her own compartment, and there inside were Uncle Lawrence and Aunt Jane. They were deep in conversation, she saw, something serious and humorless. Uncle Lawrence looked up at exactly that moment and saw Carson and Alec through the glass. His expression was impassive, and Carson felt strangely guilty, as though she'd done something wrong.

What *had* she done? Nothing, truly nothing at all. It was as though Uncle Lawrence could read her thoughts, and as though he knew that she felt an unusual rush of excitement walking through a train in Europe with a young physics tutor at Cambridge. She looked back at her uncle for an extended moment, their eyes meeting, and as this happened, Aunt Jane looked out at Carson, too. Her aunt and uncle were staring out at her just as Alec had stared out earlier from his compartment, and she was staring back just as she'd stared back at Alec earlier, only now it was *this* scene, the one inside the compartment where she supposedly belonged, that felt foreign.

Alec took Carson's arm and led her past. "Come on," he said quietly. "Let's get that much-needed air."

They walked through the remainder of first class, and then into second class, where the passengers shifted and did their best to make themselves comfortable in the seats of cramped compartments that did not open into sleeping berths. And then finally Alec opened a very heavy door and led her out onto a railed platform in the open air. The night was warm, but because the train was traveling so quickly, the rush of wind made it feel as though it was the middle of winter.

"You're shivering," said Alec.

"It's all right."

"Here," he insisted, and swiftly he removed his tweed jacket and draped it around her shoulders. She could feel the silky lining against her neck, and it was a pleasurable sensation.

"Now *you're* the one who's shivering," said Carson.

"It's all right," said Alec. "I've been a lot colder than this, believe me."

"When?" she asked.

He shrugged, making light of it. "When I was a very little boy, we didn't have much heat," he said. "Oh, we weren't penniless—I didn't have a boyhood quite like Freddy Hunt's. But my father, inasmuch as I can remember him, drank a great deal—well, he drank like a fish, as you Americans say—and there wasn't too much money left for wood to stoke the fire with, or food to eat. After he died, Mum and I made the best of it that we could. Often, Mum would take me to Mrs. Bertram's house, and it would be warm there. I'd stay inside and do my schoolwork."

"Who's Mrs. Bertram?"

Alec's face seemed to light up at the question. "Oh, she's the very wealthy lady my mum cleaned house for. Has a grand place in Bloomsbury, right near the British Museum. She's very old now, but when I was a boy she was just medium old, and I'd keep warm in her house and do my homework and she'd always tell my mum what a wonderful, hardworking lad I was." He shook his head. "All my hard work paid off, I guess, because when it came time for me to apply to college, Mrs. Bertram announced that she was planning to pay for my entire education, provided that I 'made something' with my life. My mum and I couldn't believe it! But the thing is, it changed my life. I'd never really thought about what I was going to do with myself. I was just a boy whose father was dead. Just bumming around aimlessly with my friends. But now I saw that choices *mattered*. And that I wasn't going to be a drunkard like my old man had been, or clean other people's houses like my poor mum, but that I was going to do something that made a difference in the world. So I studied physics at Cambridge, and gradually found I had a certain aptitude."

"And are you making a difference?" Carson asked.

Alec narrowed his eyes now, as if he knew exactly what he wanted out of life, as if he could see it out there in the darkness. After all the booming declarations of modesty Carson had heard back in the compartment where she'd played cards with Alec and his friends, this quiet display of certainty, of decisiveness, somehow touched her.

"I like to think I will," said Alec. Then he shook his head, and the look was gone. "But it's hard to know, so soon."

Carson wanted to reach out to him, to touch his shoulder, to tell him everything was going to be all right, that he was going to get what he wanted out of life, that he would make a difference, she was sure of it. But she felt such a gesture would be too forward, and so she turned instead and joined Alec in gazing out over the rail, as everything receded in the black night. There were distant lights belonging to houses, farms, rural people they would never meet. It all went by so quickly, Carson thought. Sights seen from a train. Life itself.

She saw now where this evening was heading. It was heading where everything always headed: toward the end. The evening would end, and Carson felt suddenly that she couldn't bear that thought. That fact of life. *This* was where she wanted to be; this was *who* she wanted to be: not a young girl, back in her bed in Connecticut, but this person in this moment now: sharing a platform with a mysterious stranger named Alec on the night train to Lisbon. A mysterious stranger herself.

"And what about you?" she heard him ask. "I've only been talking about myself. I haven't asked you a single question, and I feel terribly rude. Because the truth is that I do want to know about you, about who you are."

Carson looked away from him; she hardly knew what to say. Her own story had none of the drama that his did, and none of the dreams. "I'm not really anybody," she said softly.

"That can't be true," said Alec.

"But it is. I grew up very privileged. We had no Mrs. Bertram. My mother essentially *is* Mrs. Bertram," she said with a small laugh. "I've wanted for nothing."

"Oh, I don't believe that," said Alec.

Carson realized he was looking at her intently. What did he see in her eyes, she wondered, to cause him to make such a statement? What was missing from her gaze? She was a young woman traveling through Europe, as countless young women had done before her, and she appeared happy enough, didn't she?

"Everyone wants for something," said Alec. "Everyone has something that can't be fulfilled. It may not be money. It may be something else. Companionship. A soul mate. Friendship. Love." He spoke these words lightly, tossing them off like playing cards, making it seem as though he wasn't applying them specifically to *her*. But, of course, he was. And strangely enough, they did apply to her.

Men, her uncle had said back in London, on her first afternoon abroad, and Carson had been cautioned. But *men*, she realized now, with a shock, on this stark, cold night, wasn't the same as a single, individual *man*—one with a crooked smile, at that.

She blinked in the strange, dim light of this realization, and Alec took her face in his hand, turning it toward his. "Come here," he said, his voice a whisper, and she obeyed, moving toward him, closing her eyes as his mouth found hers and the wind lifted her hair, and the train continued on along its tracks, unaware that on the platform at its very end, a young American girl—no, a young American woman—was falling in love.

CHAPTER THREE

Disoriented from all that had happened to her aboard the night train, Carson disembarked at the Estação Santa Apolonia and stood on the crowded platform with her aunt and uncle, waiting as their luggage was unloaded by porters. The heat in Lisbon was oppressive even in the early morning, and the sunlight was far stronger than what she was used to. Though on the train there had been a stew of languages and accents, almost all the voices she heard now were speaking Portuguese, the words flying fast and becoming nearly impossible to follow. Carson hadn't slept at all last night. After Alec had kissed her, she'd been unable to calm down at all, and a little later, lying in the upper berth of her bed with her aunt below her, she'd lain wide awake, staring at the low ceiling and feeling the thudding of her own heart.

Down the corridor, Alec was lying in his own berth. Was he wide awake, too? she wondered, or was kissing a stranger on a train the sort of thing he did every day? She really had no idea at all. After the kiss, they'd stood out in the wind and simply looked at each other. Carson had felt her hair whipping around her head like a corona; she resisted the impulse to smooth it down, to make herself appear perfect.

Alec seemed to like looking at her out there with her hair so wild.

"What's going on here?" she'd asked him, as though she were a third party who'd just walked in on a kissing couple. But no, she was one half of that couple, as responsible for the kiss as he was. She'd wanted it without really knowing she'd wanted it, and it had happened. The night had been like some sort of strange fever dream, in which the dreamer finds herself walking through uncharted territory, coming upon sights she's never seen before, all of it swirling in some kind of unreal, endless, rolling mist.

But today was the day when the fever broke and the dreamer was thrust back to blinding, sun-bleached reality. Yes, she'd really kissed this man who was a total stranger. And yes, she'd really liked it. It had happened, all right. They had kissed; they had parted. Now what? Out on the platform at the station in Lisbon, Carson shielded her eyes and looked all around for him.

"What are you doing, Carson?" asked her aunt.

"It's very sunny out," Carson replied now. "I'm just shielding my eyes."

"I see."

Carson looked at her aunt, and noticed a slightly sly expression beneath the impassivity of the gaze. It was as though Jane *knew*. And maybe she did. Maybe that glimpse that Carson's aunt and uncle had gotten of Carson and Alec from their compartment was all they needed to draw their own conclusions. But before Carson had a chance to ask herself whether it mattered what her aunt and uncle might suspect, Alec appeared.

He was approaching from across the platform, lugging one end of a trunk. Freddy was carrying the other end. The two men eased the trunk to the ground, and then Alec took a step toward Carson.

"Good morning," Alec said quietly.

"Good morning." Carson heard her own voice. It sounded unnaturally shy and tentative, a tone she'd never needed to adopt with any boy back in Marlowe.

"I realized," said Alec, "that I forgot to ask where you were staying in Portugal. Will you be right in Lisbon?"

"No," said Carson. "We'll be in Sintra. We've rented a house. I mean, my aunt and uncle have."

She turned to indicate her aunt, and Carson saw that both Aunt Jane and Freddy had turned discreetly away. Did everyone know what had happened on the platform last night? Or, more likely, did they merely sense something . . . unmistakable?

"Excellent," Alec said. "My friends and I are staying right here in Lisbon, at the Pensão Moderna. But Sintra, according to my map, isn't far away at all. Many people live there and commute to Lisbon every day. Perhaps we can see each other."

"Yes, perhaps," said Carson lightly, reverting to her old Marlowe ways, acting as though such a visit might amuse when in fact it was what she wished more than anything she could recall. Unlike Harris Black or any of the boys back home, however, Alec didn't respond to her cool distance by pressing harder. Instead he responded in kind. They traded telephone numbers, and then Alec waved good-bye and headed off into the Estação Santa Apolonia with his friends, leaving Carson to watch him lug his end of the steamer trunk and to wonder whether last night's encounter had meant anything to him at all—and whether she really ever would see him again.

The roads in Portugal were both primitive and curvy as the long sedan Uncle Lawrence had rented traveled first westward, then north, to the town of Sintra. The Atlantic, along the Costa da Prata, shone blue and gold in the distance. Occasional castles appeared as if out of nowhere, the architecture old and stately. The three of them had breezed right out of Lisbon, and Carson had barely had a chance to see the city. But the coastal region was entirely different from the chic splendors of either Paris or London. Those cities were indisputably cosmopolitan, filled with shops and restaurants with gleaming silver, but this landscape was something else altogether. It wasn't about the present; it was about the past. Carson leaned back against the cracked brown leather seat and looked out through the window, silent and awed.

"You know," said Lawrence as he drove, "Lord Byron once called this town 'glorious Eden.' And in the nineteenth century it was an absolutely essential stopping place for aristocrats making the grand tour. Not unlike yourself, Carson," he added.

"Oh, stop," Jane said. "Don't tease her, Lawrie."

"I'm not teasing her."

"That's all right, Lawrence," Carson said from the backseat. Last night, after Carson had returned from her rendezvous with Alec on the train platform, her aunt had inquired before bed whether Carson could find it in herself to drop the "aunt" and "uncle" when saying their names. Now Carson sat in the rear seat of the sedan and regarded the two of them, this middle-aged couple with reservoirs of worldly experience, and wondered what form a friendship with them could possibly take. Calling either of them by their first names seemed forced. She found it difficult to imagine either of them as ever being more than chaperones—kindly and funny, but chaperones nonetheless. Even now her uncle had slipped into the role of tour guide. He had been to the region before, and as the car bumped into the village of Sintra, he pointed out the Palacio da Pena.

Carson tried to pay attention. The palacio was a Bavarian castle, her uncle was saying, and then he was saying something about Gothic turrets, and then he was saying something else about a Renaissance dome, but all the while all Carson could think about was Alec. What was he doing now? Was he settling into his hotel room in Lisbon? Was he sitting down on the bed, yawning, closing his eyes?

Was he thinking of her?

Would he ever think about her again?

She would have to put him out of her mind, she decided as the car drove ahead and her uncle continued his travelogue. Maybe the incident on the train would just become one of those memories people had, the kind they remember vaguely and fondly for many years after the fact. *The first kiss, aboard a speeding train in the continent of Europe, when I was but a girl.* Involuntarily, Carson sighed deeply, as though already being forced to turn the thought from action to memory.

From the front seat, Jane craned her head around to get a

look at Carson. "Is Lawrence boring you to death?" she asked. "If he is, don't hesitate to say so. I'll make him stop."

"Nonsense," said Lawrence. "No one has ever been bored by my travel narration."

"No one has ever admitted it, you mean," said his wife.

Carson listened to their playful marital sparring. They were a good couple, she understood, in a way that her own parents were not. Though Lawrence could be severe and distant, there was often real communication between them; it flowed like a current. And there was a parallel sexual current there, too. Though it was none of her business, she could imagine her aunt and uncle caressing each other in bed at night, whereas her own parents seemed so formal and distant. She wondered if her mother and father actually loved each other. In all her life, it had never occurred to her to wonder about this. But now it was as though her brief moment on that train had awakened her to the possibilities of a couple, to what actually being part of a couple might be like. Thinking about all of this, Carson leaned her heavy head against the glass window. There was so much to see out there, she knew, so much unfamiliar landscape and so many curious architectural details and alluring beaches and kettles of Portuguese *linguica* cooking. She was overwhelmed, and despite herself, her eyes dropped shut, and she slept.

"I think this is it," Jane was saying a little while later, and Carson awoke with a start. The car had stopped in front of a very large villa, its rough walls painted white and its roof composed of red tiles. There were flowers everywhere surrounding the house, and in the distance, the water shone.

"Welcome to the Villa do Giraldo," said Lawrence. "We hope you'll be happy here this summer, Carson."

"Oh, it's beautiful," she said, her eyes focusing, taking in the grand dimensions of the house. This was a palace of sorts, Carson thought to herself. The water was so inviting in the distance, and the house itself seemed both foreign but comfortable.

Once inside, they all toured the rooms, walking across the ubiquitous cool red stone tile. Carson's bedroom seemed like something not only from another country, but from another century. In the middle of the room was a simple white bed surrounded by a gauze netting that gave it a magical quality. On the wall above the bed hung a cross, and the walls themselves were rough and painted a simple white. Simplicity: that was the dominant sensibility at work here.

"I love it," said Carson, and as the days passed she did love it there in the Villa do Giraldo. She and Jane and Lawrence went exploring the region, stopping to make the trek up to the Palacio da Pena, and the ruins of a Moorish castle known as the Castelo dos Mouros, which loomed with seeming precariousness from the boulders high above the town proper. As Carson stood so high above the town, she looked down on all of it, and then turned so she was facing southward, toward Lisbon. Somewhere in that teeming city, Alec Breve was sitting, or walking, or eating lunch, or thinking about Carson, or not thinking about her at all.

Three days had passed since the train trip, and there had not been a word from him. Carson had been determined not to let this trouble her too much, but thoughts about him persisted, especially at night, keeping her awake as she lay beneath the veil that was draped around her bed to keep out industrious mosquitoes.

She was always traveling on that train now. The sights of Sintra, the sinful midnight suppers of crustaceans and drawn butter, her uncle's wry and vivid descriptions of the local history and architecture, the distant lapping of the waves as she lay in bed at night, the intoxicatingly salty air that greeted her with the first morning light—none of these fully distracted Carson. She might be lifting the hem of her skirt and stepping delicately across the very stones, as her uncle assured her, where navigators once stood as they stared across the Atlantic and wondered what lay on the other side, and Carson would find herself thinking instead about that night on the train. When it happened, as it happened, she had wanted it not to end, had wished she could find a way to make it last and last. And in a way, she had. That night hadn't come to an end after all. Carson was trying her best to push all thoughts of Alec from her mind, yet again and again she found herself returning to him, and flushing with the warmth of those memories, and wondering, *What if?*

What if she had allowed herself to linger longer? What if she had defied the reasonable expectation of her aunt and uncle, waiting awake back in their sleeping compartments, that their niece would return to them at a decent hour? What if she'd told Alec in that one windswept moment on the rear platform of the train how she really felt about him? What if he'd told her that he felt the same way about her?

What if she hadn't acted in such a cavalier manner toward him in the train station in Lisbon?

Stop, she told herself. *Just stop.* Those first days in Sintra she told herself this—tried to tell herself this—again and again, until she had scolded herself raw. She knew she was torturing herself, recalling over and over again that brief period on the train, the wind in her hair, the weight of Alec's jacket on her shoulders, his askew smile hovering above her, drawing nearer, until his lips parted, and then she always told herself: *Stop. Don't think about it.*

Until the night she asked herself: *Why not?*

As she lay awake within the womb of her mosquito netting, the question suddenly appeared to her. Why stop? What was the harm in thinking about the night she'd spent on the train to Lisbon? For one brief, thrilling moment, anything had seemed possible; everything had seemed perfect. The scene was like one of those fairy tales her mother had fed her before bedtime, though she didn't think her parents would exactly agree with her assessment of Alec as a prince. Still, what was the harm in reliving that moment? Why not linger on that platform in her memory in a way she hadn't allowed herself in real life? What if that kiss had in fact meant to Alec what it meant to her, and they had confessed that truth to each other, and the two of them had stepped off the train in Lisbon together, as a couple? What if Alec were beside her now, if not in this bed in her aunt and uncle's villa, then in another bed, perhaps at his *pensão*? What if the feelings, the sensations she'd experienced on the rear platform of the night train to Lisbon, could somehow last forever?

And with this happily-ever-after fairy-tale premise playing itself out in her head, Carson fell asleep.

The following morning, he telephoned. Jane answered the phone while Carson was sitting outside on the back porch, sketching the surrounding countryside, and Carson heard her aunt carrying on a friendly but slightly formal conversation. "Just a moment," Jane finally said. "I'll see if she's available."

Jane appeared outside on the porch and said quietly, "Carson, that young man is on the phone. The one from the train. You know, the one who joined us for dinner that night. Alex, I believe his name is?"

"Alec," corrected Carson, her voice betraying nothing, but within herself she was imploding. Her heart had been set racing, and when she entered the large living room now and picked up the telephone receiver, her hand shook slightly.

"Hello?"

"Is that Carson?" asked Alec. His voice sounded tinny and distant.

"Yes, it is."

"Hello there. Alec Breve speaking. Are you doing all right in Sintra? Country agreeing with you and all that?"

"Oh, yes," she said lightly. "Everything is terrific. We've been exploring the area, and it's quite interesting."

"Wish I had time to sightsee," said Alec, "but the conference keeps me busy. However, tomorrow night, it turns out, there's nothing on my schedule, and I was wondering if you were free to attend the theater with me. You may recall I mentioned there's a production of *Roméo y Julieta* here in Lisboa—I mean Lisbon. You see, I'm already picking up the local words."

"Romeo and Juliet," said Carson. "Yes, I'd really like to go. I'll have to ask permission first."

"Of course," said Alec. "You can telephone me back, if you

like, here at the Pensão Moderna. Just ask for the bookish, gangly *senhor* in room twenty-three."

"You're hardly that," Carson said before she could stop herself, and then she was embarrassed.

She hung up the phone, and closed her eyes briefly. Alec's voice hadn't been in the slightest flirtatious. He had spoken, in fact, as though they were simply two people who had met aboard the night train to Lisbon, and who had in common the fact that both of them spoke English. Perhaps that was the main feature they did share, although, as they stood out on the train platform together, their bond had been strong and undeniably sensual.

She was completely new to this sort of thing. Entanglements. Unspoken words and feelings. The way men and women were supposed to keep their true thoughts and desires hidden from the rest of the world, lest anybody find out. The subtle game that was played between interested parties. And apparently Alec *was* an interested party; apparently the kiss hadn't been a disaster. She'd kissed him like she'd meant it, because she had meant it. It hadn't taken any dissembling on her part.

But later on that night, at dinner with her aunt and uncle in the plaza downtown in Sintra, sitting under the moon, the palm fronds rubbing lightly together all around them, a band of mariachis seranading the tables with a mournful rendition of "Manha de Carnaval," Carson felt she ought to present her desire to meet Alec in Lisbon in as light and casual a way as possible.

"So," she said as she selected a morsel of *escabeche*—local uncooked fish delicately marinated in lime juice—and raised it to her mouth, "I've been invited to a Shakespeare play."

"Ah. The bard himself. I knew him well," said Lawrence, and it took Carson half a moment before she realized he was paraphrasing a line from Shakespeare. He looked at her across the table with its white cloth and glittering glasses half filled with local white sangria and floating chunks of apple and melon. "I'm glad you'll be getting some culture this summer," he continued drily. "I know how important that is to you." And then he drained his glass.

Carson pretended not to notice the irony at work here. But clearly Lawrence was slightly uncomfortable with Carson going off to the city with a man she'd just met on the train. *What would your mother think?* That was the subtext of Lawrence's concern, though he hadn't said a word. Aunt Jane didn't offer an opinion, though Carson secretly hoped—and suspected—that her aunt was rooting her on. After all, Aunt Jane had been just a year beyond Carson's current age when she'd traveled abroad and fallen in love with an English civil servant. Carson had grown up hearing from her mother how Aunt Jane had shocked the entire family when she'd announced that she loved this young Brit named Lawrence Emmett, and that they were planning to be married. Carson's own mother, Philippa, had taken the safer course, marrying Arthur Weatherell, whom the entire family knew and approved of, and who was sure to provide well for her. But Lawrence Emmett was an unknown, an X factor from the other side of the ocean, and no one had known what to expect of him. Happily, the marriage had worked out well, and no one ever complained again, but surely Jane could still remember what tensions she'd created in her own family when she'd fallen in love with someone who hadn't been approved of in advance.

And surely, too, Jane was looking across the dinner table at her niece with something approaching admiration. "Honestly, Lawrie," Jane murmured. "Leave the poor girl alone. She's just trying to have a little fun. You remember fun, don't you? It's spelled *F-U-N*, and it tends to happen to young people, *if* they're lucky."

"Don't patronize me, Jane," said her husband. "We promised your sister that we'd protect Carson this summer, not expose her to all kinds of people we know nothing about."

"Oh, but we do know about him," said Jane. "I found him to be perfectly charming, and I thought you did, too."

Lawrence grumbled something that Carson couldn't hear, because just at that moment, the mariachis reached a climactic moment in their ballad, and the guitars were suddenly strummed very loudly. But the upshot of the discussion was that Carson would apparently be allowed to attend the Shakespeare play with Alec in Lisbon, provided he return her to the villa by midnight.

"Or else my coach will turn into a pumpkin?" Carson teased her aunt and uncle.

"Something like that," that Lawrence, and she could see a smile playing on the edges of his lips. "All right, all right," he conceded. "I suppose I am a worrywart. But we've been entrusted with your care this summer, and you're still quite young."

"I know that, Lawrence," Carson said. She had begun to enjoy casting the word *uncle* aside. She'd decided that it made her feel far more sophisticated than she really was.

"But what else is being young for," put in Jane, "if not for moments like these?"

So the following day, Carson boarded a local train in the center of Sintra and traveled to Lisbon. This time, she sat in a compartment full of well-dressed and proper Portuguese men and women. No one spoke English, and all the men smoked. Though Carson was just beginning to pick up some of the language—*ola* for "hello," and *obrigado* for "thank you," and *Quanto custa?* for the tourist's most necessary question, "How much does this cost?"—the culture still felt exotic, yet she wasn't anxious. She had somewhere to go, and someone who was meeting her there.

Sure enough, barely an hour later, there he was at the Rossio train station in Lisbon, standing out on the boiling platform in the same suit jacket and shirt he'd worn on the train, tieless and open-collared, his face a high color, his expression expectant. He squinted out at the train as it slowly chugged into the station with a few sluggish blasts of steam and soot, and then ground to a halt.

"You came," Alec said as he took her hand and helped her down off the metal stairs.

"You didn't think I would?" she asked.

"Wasn't sure," he admitted. "Actually, I thought it was rather impressive that you'd said yes in the first place. But whether or not you'd really show up—well, that was another point entirely. But I had faith," he went on as he led her through the station. Here and there, vendors were selling bunches of local flowers in cones of newsprint, and small paper bags of freshly fried almonds, the hot oil seeping through the bag, and brightly colored scoops of ice cream, known here as *sorveto*.

Once out of the Estação Rossio, they strolled through the

maze of small streets together, passing through the Baixa section, Lisbon's old business district, with elegant buildings and stone streets, heading toward the Tague River, where they stopped by the rail and looked out for a few moments. Alec bought Carson and himself some lemon soda, and the two of them held the small greenish bottles in their hands and drank and talked shyly.

"Do you like Portugal?" he asked.

"Oh, yes," she said immediately. "Though I haven't seen much yet. Just what my uncle and aunt have shown me. A bit of local tourism and the antiquities of Sintra. Moorish castles, very beautiful. And in a few days we're all going to the beach. How about you?" she asked.

"Well, I haven't seen very much either," said Alec. "Mostly I've been in conferences. Not very exciting, I'm afraid. Lots of blowhards from around the world, speaking through simultaneous interpreters. But I'm giving my little lecture tomorrow. Think I'd better do something to liven it up. I don't know, maybe I should use hand puppets in my presentation, what do you think?"

Carson laughed. "Hand puppets, definitely," she said. "And musical accompaniment, too, I hope."

"Definitely music," Alec agreed. "In fact, I'm hiring a mariachi band. They'll play that famous, sentimental, international favorite, 'Electrical Conductors and Alternating-Current Receptivity.' "

They both laughed easily together, before beginning to talk more seriously. "Are you nervous?" she asked, referring to the lecture.

He paused, looking at her, considering the question. "A

little, I think," he finally said. "I've spoken in public before, but only to groups of well-wishers, never anybody particularly important. It's not that this conference is bound to make my name, exactly . . . though if my paper goes over poorly, it certainly will be a bit of a blow."

"I'm sure it won't go over poorly," said Carson.

"How do you know?" he asked.

"I can tell."

There was a pause, and then Alec asked her, "Are *you* nervous?"

She was thrown by the question for a moment, for of course she wasn't going to be presenting a paper, but then she understood that he was asking her if she was nervous right now. Here, with him.

Carson was aware that she actually felt comfortable with Alec. Her nervousness had dissipated. If he were to kiss her again today, she would not be as shocked as she'd been on the train. She hoped he *would* kiss her again; now that he'd called, now that they were together again, she rather expected that he was going to do so before the day was over. Oddly, a sense of calm flooded her.

"No," she said to him. "I'm not nervous."

"Good," said Alec. "I'm glad." Then he took her hand and led her away from the water. They hopped on a bus and headed to the Bairro Alto, an area of the city that was heavily populated by young Portuguese men and women. The neighborhood was anything but fancy; there were plenty of narrow streets and flights of stone stairs and Baroque churches, mixed in with little stores. A fish vendor called out the exotic names of his wares on a corner, and three fat ladies dressed in widow's black hovered around his cart, examining the merchandise. In a small jewelry shop called Fragil, Carson admired a simple bracelet with blue beads, and Alec immediately bought it for her.

"No, no," she protested, but he insisted. The bracelet was inexpensive, but Carson knew that Alec lived on a tutor's wage, and that money surely was scant. She had her own money with her; her parents had sent her to Europe well prepared. But she didn't want to make him feel bad, and so she accepted the gift. They stood outside on the Rua de Carmo while he opened the clasp and slipped it onto her wrist. The tiny blue beads looked beautiful against her slender white arm.

"Lovely," he said quietly, and Carson just nodded.

After they'd wandered the city and shopped some more (Carson bought candles for her aunt and uncle, as well as soap and perfume for her parents), then stopped in a café for iced, sweet Portuguese coffee, the sky darkened and they made their way to a restaurant that Alec said he'd read about in his Baedeker guidebook. "It's supposed to be excellent," he said. "Wonderful seafood, the book said."

What the Baedeker had not said about the Restaurante Estrela do Chiado was that it was also a very romantic spot. Carson and Alec had their meal on the patio out back, beneath the stars and a line of laundry hanging distantly from a building high above, and the sounds of children's voices echoing in the evening. The tables were spaced far enough apart to give the diners their privacy. Carson and Alec sat facing each other, speaking only when they really wanted to. The occasional waves of silence did not really need to be filled; Carson and Alec were simply enjoying being together at this table, in this place. Food was almost an afterthought. Carson realized that she hadn't thought once all day about that night on the train. She didn't need to now. Now she was here, with him.

"I've heard that there is a local classic dish in Lisbon," Alec finally told her when the waiter had brought their menus, "called *bacalhau cozido com grao e batatas.*"

"It sounds exotic," said Carson.

"Not really," Alec said. "It's just codfish, chickpeas, and potatoes. Ingredients that you have eaten separately before in America, I presume, but the combination is supposed to be pretty great."

They both ordered the *bacalhau,* and it was garlicky and delicious, and when they were done and Alec had paid the bill, they headed toward the nearby outdoor amphitheater for the Shakespeare performance. There was a preponderance of couples in attendance, Carson realized as they took their seats on curved, rustic wooden bleachers. All around her, other young men and women sat closely, arms entwined. She and Alec, they weren't a couple, not really, but here at this theater, everyone who saw them would certainly think they were. *We look good together,* Carson thought. She was delicate-boned, blond, and fair-skinned, and he was darker, brown-haired, and angular.

When the play started, Carson noted that "Julieta" had the same coloring that she did, and that "Roméo" was built more along Alec's lines, his hair brown and hanging in his face a bit. Alec couldn't have failed to notice this either, Carson thought, and as they sat side by side on the hard wood, intently watching the production on the distant stage being spoken in a language that was completely incomprehensible to either of them, he took her hand in his, his fingers playing with the tiny blue beads of the bracelet he'd bought her. Something stirred inside her.

It was during the balcony scene, when Julieta was asking "Wherefore art thou, Romeo?"—or, at least, the Portuguese version of the question—that Alec lifted Carson's hand up to his mouth and gently kissed each finger. Then he stroked her fingers there in the dark, and slowly took each one and placed the tip lightly in his mouth for a mere second. The feelings that this created inside Carson were powerful, unlike anything she had felt before. His mouth was on her littlest finger now; he sucked the fingertip gently, and Carson involuntarily closed her eyes. *Wherefore art thou Romeo?* When she was a younger girl and had first read the play in school, she and almost everyone else in her class at Miss Purslane's had understood the line to mean, "Where are you, Romeo?" It had seemed to be the question of a young lover calling beseechingly into the darkness. But no, their kindly old teacher, Mr. Benjamin, had explained that the line actually meant, "*Why* are you called Romeo?" It meant what, in essence, was the meaning of the label, the name, when Romeo's true essence lay not in such a label, but in *himself?*

Wherefore art thou Alec? she wondered to herself now as he kissed and caressed her hand. He was someone she did not really know; they had met on a night train to Lisbon, two travelers from different countries, drawn together by something she did not understand. Certainly, it was called attraction; that much she knew. But possibly, just possibly, Carson thought as Alec leaned toward her now, tipping her face up to meet his own, the two of them looking for a long moment into each other's eyes, the amphitheater blurring and disappearing, along with the actors and the audience, and the ticket sellers, and the trees, and the city in the distance, it was also called love. *Amoro*. Yes, that was what it was, Carson knew, and she trusted her instincts, and wasn't afraid.

Wherefore art thou Alec? It didn't matter really, not one bit. He was someone strange and new, but, improbably, he was hers.

CHAPTER FOUR

So then they were in love. Full-flowering, astonishing love, the kind that Carson had always read about—the kind, she supposed, that her mother had hoped she would one day have with Harris Black back in Connecticut. Could people even really fall in *love* in Connecticut? she wondered, for here in Portugal the atmosphere seemed somehow to enhance her love for Alec Breve. She and Alec held hands as they strolled through the old streets of the city or the Praça Dom Pedro IV, the city's main square, listening to the tolling of distant bells. They stole kisses as they wandered the windswept rocky coastline of Sintra, the spray of the ocean crashing far below. They explored the beaches of gorgeous Cascais, where tanned and well-rested couples lay splayed on the fine sand, couples just like themselves.

This *was* a fairy tale, in a way, Carson realized. That first moment on the train, when Carson glanced into a smoky compartment and Alec Breve glanced up from his playing cards and their eyes met: wasn't that love at first sight—or at least as close as it comes in real life? That whole headlong rush all evening on board the train, as if their bodies were willing them toward that platform and a kiss born of urgency as much as passion: wasn't that a now-or-never moment—a perfect example of two lives taking a sudden turn that neither lover could have possibly foreseen but afterward acquires the inevitability of dream logic?

So Alec was to be her prince. He just wasn't the kind of prince her mother would approve of, Carson suspected. Sometimes when Carson and Alec strolled, and a silence filled the space between them that neither felt the need to fill, that both in fact allowed to linger, the better to slow the passage of time, she would try to imagine the moment she would introduce Alec to her parents. Carson wouldn't even have to explain; her parents would just *sense* that Alec wasn't one of their own. Her mother would be gracious toward Alec, of course, but Carson would detect in her eyes a surprise mingled with disappointment, and then later her father would pull her aside to quietly inquire just how much she trusted this poor English chap—how she could be absolutely sure Alec wasn't simply some gold digger with designs on the Weatherell family fortune. In those moments of silent reflection, Carson would find herself sighing inwardly and wishing that her parents could somehow be as understanding, as accepting—as open to life's life-altering possibilities—as Jane and Lawrence. And then Carson would turn to Alec and give his hand a squeeze, as if he were the one in need of reassurance.

For as improbable a prince as Alec might seem in her parents' estimation, Carson seemed just as unlikely a princess in her own. Sure, her good looks and easy grace and offhand flirtatiousness might be the ideal complement to the likes of Harris Black, but what did she have to offer the likes of Alec Breve? He didn't care about money. He didn't need a wife who could oversee a dinner party for twenty without breaking a sweat. He didn't want everything that Carson Weatherell had been taught, for as long as she could remember, men wanted.

So what *did* he want? He wanted the thrill of the chase as he tracked down the subtleties of a physics equation. He wanted the satisfaction that comes from cobbling a life, however improvised, out of mathematics and cigarettes and camaraderie. But most of all what Alec Breve wanted, as improbable as it sometimes seemed to Carson, was her.

And so in the days following that evening of *bacalhau* and Shakespeare, they strolled, and they wandered, and they explored, and then one day Alec took Carson on a bus to the very westernmost point of the entire European continent, Cabo da Roca, and there, at a small *pensão*, they made love.

They had arranged to go there in advance; he'd brought the subject up tentatively, trying to gauge how she would respond. What he'd said was, "Carson, I want to be with you."

"You are with me," she'd said. They were sitting on the porch of her aunt and uncle's villa at the time, side by side on the porch swing, her head in his lap, and he was stroking her blond spill of hair. Both Lawrence and Jane were well out of earshot.

"No, I want to be *with* you," he tried again, his voice quieter, even shy. "I don't know how you'll react to this, and God knows I don't want to scare you off, but I'll say it anyway." He paused, then said, "I want to make love to you. I want it so much."

"Oh," she said, and she quickly looked away. Of course she wanted this, too, but it was not what she was supposed to want, not even remotely, and as a result, the mutuality of their feelings alarmed her. Whom could she talk to about all of this? Her aunt? Although their "friendship" had developed over the past weeks, Jane was still and forever her "aunt," no matter by what name Carson called her. No, Carson had no one. No one but him.

Alec was whom she'd come to confide in. Alec was the confidant, the constant companion, the endless receptacle into which she could pour her wishes and desires and dreams. Even though their lives were so different—or maybe *because* their lives were so different—the fact was, she could talk to him, and he to her, about almost anything. When she spoke of her upbringing, and her fairy-tale existence, he seemed to understand, nodding at key moments and asking all kinds of incisive questions, trying his hardest to imagine what this "Connecticut" must be like. And he seemed to understand, too, her embarrassment or discomfort or even boredom at having to describe dinners at the country club, the intricacies of the social season, the charity work that seemed to speak more to the needs of the wealthy women stuffing envelopes and ordering arrangments of flowers than those of the disadvantaged they were helping. And so he would gently switch subjects and talk instead about *her*—who Carson was—in a way that nobody else ever had. *Who was your very best friend?* he wanted to know. *When were you happiest? What's been your deepest fear?*

And when it was her turn, she would try to learn what his "Cambridge" must be like, and she, too, soon learned that he didn't want to be defined only by equations on a blackboard. It was when he spoke of his own childhood, describing in detail his memories of his father, his relationship with his mother, now deceased, and the elderly, wealthy woman named Mrs. Violet Bertram whose house she'd cleaned, who had sent Alec to Cambridge, and who still maintained a room for him in her house—when he spoke of all this, he spoke from the heart, and Carson listened, rapt.

Maybe they weren't so different after all. Maybe this is what they had in common: Carson and Alec had come from isolated lives, they had always thought that in some way, without even thinking about it, how they lived was how the rest of the world lived, and now they knew otherwise. *What else?* one of them would ask, and the amazing thing was that there always *was* something else, something more, another detail or story that he could summon, or that she could remember about her own childhood, one more round of memories that they could share, and in so doing, remain together a little while longer.

They were getting to know each other; this was what people in love did. It happened effortlessly, and the more that Carson learned about Alec, the more she seemed to love him, and when he asked her to make love with him, it was him she naturally wanted to ask about whether she should. But she couldn't, and so she had to do once more what she'd found herself doing so often during this endlessly surprising and suddenly consequential summer, and decide for herself.

"Yes," she whispered.

Her aunt and uncle, upon realizing that their niece was falling in love while under their care, were of course concerned. "You're a young girl," Lawrence said that very same night at dinner, "and he's an older man."

"Not so old. He's twenty-five," said Carson.

"But compared with you, it's a lifetime," Lawrence grumbled.

"Ignore your uncle," said Jane. "He's forgotten what it was like to woo me when I was but a girl myself. The age difference shouldn't really matter if you truly and honestly get to know and respect each other."

"Thank you," said Carson.

"If, of course," Jane added lightly, "you're well aware of what you're getting into: that a man in his twenties might expect the relationship to include certain elements that are, shall we say, inappropriate for a girl your age."

Jane looked at her niece sternly, and Carson found herself simply looking back, not wavering or blinking. What was happening between herself and Alec was something so exciting that she wanted to talk about it with everyone, to climb to the top of a Moorish castle and shout it over the hills, and yet she also knew that she could not do that. Her aunt and uncle would not approve. No one she knew would. If her own parents found out that she was falling in love with a penniless English physicist in his twenties who had just this afternoon whispered to her, "I want to make love to you," they would personally fly over to Portugal and drag her home, making sure that she never saw him again.

So she wouldn't tell anyone. She would keep it between herself and Alec, where it rightfully belonged. She would travel with him the following day, as they'd planned, to Cabo da Roca, and enter the *pensão* posing as man and wife.

And so it was in that *pensão* that Carson found herself sitting on a simple white bed facing a window that overlooked the sea and the west. Across that great expanse, far, far away, were Carson's parents, just waking up and having their coffee and toast and eggs-over-easy, for in America it was still morning. But here in Portugal, time had already passed and it was the middle of the afternoon, and Alec Breve was sitting down beside her on the bed.

"You are so lovely," he said, and she lowered her eyes, then began to unbutton her blouse. Her hands were shaking so hard, she could barely undo the tiny seed-pearl buttons. "Are you cold?" he asked, concerned, but she shook her head no. "Just scared?" She nodded. "Don't be, darling," he said. "Please." He kissed her cheek and stroked her hair.

"I'm trying not to be," said Carson.

"If this isn't what you want, we can wait," Alec said. "We can wait as long as you want."

"No," she said. "I don't want to wait." She wanted to touch him, wanted to see his body, tanned from the Portuguese sun, free of its clothes. She wanted to see the muscles in his legs and arms, and look into his eyes in the dim afternoon light. She wanted him as much as he wanted her.

And then, to her own surprise as well as his, she opened her blouse fully and pulled him against her, lying back onto the bed and bringing him atop her, so she could feel the weight of his body on hers. He actually felt *weightless*, she realized, and even the bed itself seemed unmoored from the floor in this small, simple room. They began kissing each other quickly and urgently, and touching each other everywhere, exploring, trying it all out, creating delicate patterns with hands and mouths, and as if from some great distance she heard a voice say "Oh, don't stop," and she had no idea whether it was his voice speaking, or her own.

. . .

Later, back on the bus to Lisbon, the couple sat side by side for a long while, barely speaking but simply letting themselves think back over what had just happened, and where this would all lead. For Carson, making love with Alec was the most extraordinary experience she'd ever had. The woven straw seat of the bus was hard and uncomfortable, and the vehicle itself seemed to have been manufactured in an entirely different era. A woman in the seat behind them carried a live chicken on her lap; it continually squawked and complained and shrugged its feathers into the air throughout the short trip into the city.

At one point Alec turned to Carson and looked at her. "Are you all right now?" he asked.

"Yes," she said.

"Good," he said. "I wanted to make sure you weren't feeling . . . regret, or something like that."

"No," she said. "Not at all."

She knew that he'd been with other women; he'd told her so when she'd asked. He'd been embarrassed by the question but had answered it as honestly as he could. Yes, he'd said, he had been with women before, three to be exact, but none of them had really amounted to anything in the end. Two of them were fellow students at Cambridge, one studying history, the other mathematics; the third was an older woman, a barmaid he'd met at a party right after he graduated. He hadn't loved any of them. With Carson it was different, he said. With Carson he'd felt everything it seemed humanly possible to feel. Though the experience of lovemaking was new to her and not to him, he'd explained that it did feel new to him when he was with her, because it was the first time that it had *counted*. It was the first time he'd ever been in love with the woman he was making love to. And she knew he was telling her the truth.

Today he would go to his scientific conference and she would return to Sintra. Tonight he would have dinner with Freddy and Tom and Michael, and she would sit across from her aunt and uncle in the Villa do Giraldo.

How was your trip to Cabo da Roca? they would want to know.

Oh, fine, fine. Would you pass the salad, please?

Of course. And what did you see there, Carson? Any particularly interesting sights?

Oh yes. A beautiful man, stretched out naked on a white bed.

Short of saying such things to them, she really had nothing to tell. There would be a strained silence between herself and Jane and Lawrence, Carson knew. She needed time to figure out how to manage all of this.

"You know," said Alec as the bus passed a massive collection of stones that formed the vague outline of a castle, long abandoned, "we only have two weeks more."

"I know," she said, and she could hear a note of surprise in her voice, even though the number of days they had left to spend together was something she thought about often.

"I want to see you all the time," Alec went on. "And when those two weeks are over, and then you go back to the States . . ." Here his voice faded out.

"Yes?" Carson asked, leaning against his shoulder.

"I'd like to find a way to come visit you there, to be near

you. Maybe even get myself a visiting teaching appointment for the spring term. That is, if you'd like that." She turned to study his face and saw there the sincerity, even the open vulnerability, in his expression. "Of course," he added quickly, "it's probably way too soon to be thinking about permanence in a serious way. I wasn't pushing for marriage yet, because you're young, and that would be folly, but I hoped that we could remain close to each other until we're ready for such a commitment. I have no idea of what the world holds," he went on. "This German business is extremely worrying, and if it grows more serious, then it could even come to war."

"Do you really think it will?" she said, and she heard the same note of surprise in her voice as when she'd acknowledged that hers and Alec's time together was drawing to a close—as if the possibility of war were also a presence that she couldn't deny, but couldn't bear to acknowledge either.

"Well," said Alec. "I'm not sure. Not that my opinion counts for anything. Your uncle would have a better grasp of the situation. You should ask him."

"Well, I think he's quite dire about it," she said. "You're right, I should," she added, but she knew she probably wouldn't. The fact was, if the difficulties in Europe had all seemed so distant and remote from her while she'd been living her privileged life back in Connecticut, they had seemed paradoxically even more so here, as she was falling in love with Alec.

"Look, my love," Alec suddenly said, "we can't possibly know what's going to happen in the world, and probably nothing *will* happen." He gave her shoulder a squeeze, as if trying to shield her as long as he could—as long as they were together. "The last war, the Great War, was so horrible, it's difficult to believe the world would be willing to go through another one. Surely we've all learned lessons from it. Surely no one will want to make the same mistakes. What I want to say now has nothing to do with war. It has to do with us. How much I love being with you."

"Thank you," was all Carson could say.

"Listen," he went on. "I've put off saying this as long as I could. I'm sorry, darling, but I can't be with you tomorrow. I really must prepare for the delivery of my paper at the evening session. But I'll be thinking of you all day—"

"I'll come," Carson suddenly said. "To the conference. To see you deliver your paper."

"Oh, don't be silly. You'll be bored to tears."

"Not if you're delivering it."

"Well, it's very sweet of you to offer, but really, I must confess, I'm not thinking only of your well-being here. I'm afraid you'd be too much of a distraction for me."

"Oh," she answered.

"Frankly," continued Alec, "it's bad enough as it is, being with you all the time. Bad for my work, I mean. I haven't been able to concentrate on a word of my conference. The other fellows tell me I seem like I'm in a daze. And I guess I am."

"Me, too," she said. "Here I am away from America for the first time in my life, and I can barely pay attention to any of the sights. All I can think about all the time is how much I want to be with you."

He kissed her cheek. "You're my kind of tourist," he said, and then the bus rolled into Lisbon, and it was time to get off.

The following days passed in a kind of blur, as though seen

from the window of a train—or perhaps from the rear platform, on a passionate night, as life sweeps past and all you can do is try to think of a way to make it all stop, to make life and time stand still, to make one stolen moment last forever. The delivery of his paper had gone well, Alec reported back to Carson by telephone. He was almost giddy as he described to her how he'd been reassured by the experience, how he was beginning to believe, perhaps for the first time, that he had something to contribute to his discipline. But the best news of all, he added as Carson listened, twisting the telephone cord around one finger as if she were nervously playing with a lock of her hair, was that now he was all hers.

Carson would take the local bus from Sintra to downtown Lisbon, and he would be waiting for her on the street. As the bus approached, she would often look out and see him there in his white shirt, sleeves rolled up, dark hair falling in his face, and she would feel a tremendous flush of excitement, because, just as Alec had said on the telephone, he *was* hers— as surely as she was his. She would hurry down the bus steps into the street and into his arms, and they would walk for a while, linked together, heads close, whispering into each other's ear, saying nothing and everything all at once. They stopped in at shops and got each other small gifts: he bought her a pale yellow-and-red shawl, and she bought him a wallet made of extremely soft, buttery leather.

Sometimes they sat in a *confeitaria* and ate local pastries; a particular favorite was olive-oil cake, rich and golden, with almonds studding the top like buttons on a sofa. Alec introduced Carson to the delicacy known as the blood orange, which had a complex, perfumed taste and a bright red interior. How odd that something so innocent and ordinary look-ing, like an orange, could conceal such a surprise within. Car-son's high-school English class had studied metaphors, and she realized that this was kind of a metaphor for herself: she was a fairly ordinary, privileged Connecticut girl, yet in fact she was in possession of desires and longings and passions that were invisible on the outside. Only when you got inside who she was—when you were able to capture her heart, as Alec had done—did these qualities reveal themselves.

In the afternoon, when they were done walking and day-dreaming in cafés and it was time for siesta, the entire city shut down and Carson and Alec would slip into his room at the Pensão Moderna. There they would lie together on the narrow, clean bed in the room with the simple writing desk and Alec's Dopp kit on the bureau, and make love slowly, ten-derly, as though they had all the time in the world, when in fact they did not. Sometimes, when they were through with their lovemaking and it was quiet and drowsy in the room, Carson would go to the window and sit on the ledge for a few moments, looking down over the Rua 1 de Decembro. Siesta was just ending; people were returning from their homes, re-freshed, and going back to work, to school, to shop at the open-air markets. Carson saw women carrying bread, and a man with a basket of gleaming silver fish on his head; she heard cathedral bells somewhere and a dissonant car horn honking. Although time seemed to stand still in this small room, outside it was moving forward, and complicated lives were being lived by people who could go about their business as if they had all the time in the world, because, in a way, they did. They lived here. Whatever life they'd made for themselves, they had the luxury of living it without knowing that in a matter of days they would be leaving it behind.

"I have to go," Carson always said reluctantly.

The last bus back to Sintra left at 4:15 P.M., and it was important that she be home in time for dinner, or else her aunt and uncle would become upset. It was an unspoken rule that she should be there as often as she could for dinner, at least to give the illusion of a cohesive family unit, the three members of which knew one another's whereabouts, when in fact Jane and Lawrence had no idea of how she and Alec spent their afternoons.

Or maybe they did know. If they did, they weren't saying. They'd been fairly liberal with her, despite Lawrence's grousing, allowing her this "summer romance," as Jane had put it, and knowing full well that she'd be leaving Portugal, and Europe itself, in less than a week. What they didn't know was that Alec wanted to follow her back to the States in a few months. Carson couldn't imagine how they would react if they knew how serious the relationship had become. She was afraid of their response, afraid that they would cable her parents, and so she tried hard to act casual whenever the subject of Alec Breve came up.

In the hallway outside his room at the *pensão* one afternoon, Alec was accompanying Carson down the hallway, when they happened upon Michael Morling and Freddy Hunt.

"Well, hullo," Michael said, trying not to demonstrate any sort of reaction upon finding Alec with Carson there, the couple so transparently in a postlovemaking state in the middle of the afternoon. "How have you been, Carson?" Michael asked, but he was blushing furiously.

"Fine, just fine," said Carson.

"I can see that," said Freddy with an undisguised smirk.

"Oh, shut up, Hunt, and act your age, for once," said Alec with surprising annoyance. "Fourteen, isn't it?"

"Look," said Freddy, "I didn't mean anything by it. I'm just glad that you two found each other again, and that you're happy, that's all. How about all of us going out for some *vinho?*"

"Are you allowed to drink, sport?" asked Alec.

"Ha-ha. But the real question is, is *Carson* allowed to?" countered Freddy.

Touché. Despite every reason not to, Carson liked Freddy Hunt. He had a spark of life about him, a whimsicality that you didn't expect to find in a scientist. Alec was often very serious, which suited him, but Freddy provided an air of play that helped serve as a breather to Carson, who threatened to be overwhelmed by the intensity of her affair with Alec.

The foursome went out to a bar called João, where they ordered a round of sweet but subtly potent Brazilian *caipiroscas*. There was still a little time left before the bus was leaving for Sintra, and though Carson would have been underage back home, no one here cared. Everyone drank, young and old. One drink and one drink only was what she allowed herself; even though no one was watching her, she still felt compelled to be *good*. She had lost her virginity this summer; she didn't want to lose herself as well, and so was determined to be rational and clearheaded about every experience and decision.

The *caipirosca* did loosen her up a little, at least verbally, and she found herself willing to talk to Alec's friends about her life in America. They were curious about what it was like there.

"They tell me," said Freddy, "that many people in the

States have been getting worked up about Germany as well. Is that your experience?"

"It does come up pretty often at dinner at home," Carson said. "And of course it's all over the papers. But if my father had *really* been worried, he wouldn't have sent me abroad. So I guess until I came to Europe, I didn't understand the magnitude of the topic. The reality of it."

"It feels *unreal*, in a way," said Michael. "Back home, the British Union of Fascists has been making lots of noise. You know, Oliver Mosley's crowd. He's the one who fell in love with that Mitford girl. It amazed me that she could go for that, and that her conscience doesn't stop her, doesn't stop *any* of these people. And yet people keep taking them seriously. And then there's Germany, and Italy. People seem to be in the mood to take any number of ridiculous ideas seriously."

"I know," agreed Freddy. "It's like some monster has gotten loose and wants to conquer the world. Like King Kong."

"Oh, I loved that movie," said Carson, and immediately she felt foolish, as if she were actually more interested in Hollywood than Hitler.

"Speaking of movies," Michael said to Carson, "have you by any chance ever met Clark Gable? I think he's smashing."

"No." Carson laughed. "I live in Connecticut, not California. Our paths are very unlikely to ever cross. Except in the downtown movie theater, that is, with him on the screen and me in the balcony."

"I'd like to be in that balcony with you," Alec said under his breath. "Maybe I will, in the winter," and Carson squeezed his hand under the table.

Suddenly Freddy raised his glass into the air, slightly sloshing his drink over the edge. "Hear, hear," he said. "To our old pal Alec Breve, brainy thermal physicist, and his beautiful American girlfriend. Carson," Freddy added, smiling warmly at her, "may you forever raise the thermal level of Alec, so that you may keep each other warm throughout your lives."

Everyone raised their glasses and drank.

Carson realized that the secret of her and Alec's love was slowly being nudged from its hiding place. Two of his closest friends knew about it, and surely Tom, the fourth friend, would hear about it later. These young men seemed accepting of Carson's role in Alec's life; they had seen him with women before, and they themselves had perhaps been in love with women. Love was something to be celebrated, to lift your glasses to, and not to be hidden away with a sense of shame. There was something about being here in Portugal, in this country with its mournful, romantic strum of guitars and Latin blood and sensual language—Portuguese was considered a *Romance* language, after all—that generated images of lovers throughout the ages lingering in cafés and under the moon at night, and in the darkened corners of Moorish castles.

If Carson and Alec had met back in the States, they might never have fallen in love. Surely setting played an important role in this kind of intense chemistry. Even that night train, clattering across the rails of France and Spain and then into Portugal, had been mysterious and romantic, awakening in her a kind of yearning that she hadn't known existed. She understood, now, a bit of what was happening—that sometimes you needed to go far away from home in order to find a sense of belonging. It was one of the tritest concepts in the world, and yet it applied perfectly to Carson's situation.

How could she be without him? She could, but she didn't want to. He was right; he would have to come be with her in Connecticut in the winter.

And yet, and yet . . .

As she looked from face to face around this table, she knew that his friends had started to become part of her, too. What if she didn't return home, but in fact stayed on in Europe? What if she and Alec lived together in England? They'd have no money, but so what? There were other things that mattered more than material possessions. In the back of her mind she heard the words *Fascists* and *Germany* and *Nazi Party* and *war,* which all served as a kind of Greek chorus to remind her of the real dangers that existed here in Europe, but somehow she didn't believe them. They seemed so far away from this idyllic spot, this tiny café called João, where the *caipiroscas* went down sweet and easy.

Later, at the bus stop, Alec kissed her dozens of times, unwilling to part, wanting to taste her lips one final time, even though they would be seeing each other the next afternoon.

"I love you, I love you, I love you," he said quietly, playfully, but still with a sense of urgency.

"You're drunk, Alec," said Carson.

"Yes, I know," he said, lightly playing with the blue-beaded bracelet on her wrist, turning it around and around. "But it doesn't matter. With or without the drinks, I still love you. You know I do."

"Yes," she said, pressing him harder against her. "I know."

When the old bus arrived at the stop and Carson stepped on, Alec held her hand for one second and spoke a single incomprehensible line in Portuguese.

"What's that mean?" she asked.

" 'Parting is such sweet sorrow,' " he said.

Moving from the bliss of being with Alec to the far more mundane environment of her aunt and uncle's household was no small feat. After the bus pulled into Sintra, Carson had hurried home, arriving just in time for dinner.

"Ah, Carson, good, you're here," called Jane as her niece pushed open the heavy front door of the villa. "I could use a little help with the salad, if you don't mind."

The comment was said lightly and without the slightest audible trace of annoyance, yet somehow Carson felt there was a bit of pointed criticism beneath her benign words. After Carson freshened up, she entered the kitchen, smoothly going to stand beside Jane at the counter and begin to chop vegetables for the salad. She held the small knife in her hand and let the blade fall repeatedly against the head of lettuce and the onion, trying to appear casual and nonchalant, but she realized that her hand was shaking slightly.

"So," Carson said, "what did you do today, Jane?"

"Oh, not much," her aunt admitted. "Lawrence received a telegram, of all things; I guess his work never really does end, does it, even when he's on vacation. We had been planning to take a picnic lunch out to the beach, and perhaps get some sun and surf, but oh, no, he decided he suddenly *had* to respond to the telegram by making a telephone call. And the telephone service here is so primitive—it's practically two cups and some string—so it took him forever to get a line abroad. He had to wait for the operator, and that took practically all afternoon. So my lovely picnic was ruined. I had bought some *bacalhau*, and some delicious local olives, too. Oh, well."

Carson looked up at her aunt and realized that her expression wasn't one of disapproval toward Carson, but rather discontent with her own life right now, with having a husband who was often unavailable, even on vacation.

"I'm sorry," Carson said softly. "You must have been very disappointed."

"Well, I was, I suppose," said Jane. "It's silly, isn't it? You marry someone and expect your relationship to be as romantic as it was the day you first met. You tell yourself it will be, that you two will be different. But then work slowly and surely gets in the way. It always does, especially when you're married to someone who works for one of the ministries."

"Tell you what," said Carson suddenly. "Tomorrow, let's you and I do something together." She would have to call Alec and break their date for the afternoon, and then one more day would be crossed off the calendar before he left Carson and returned to Cambridge. But Carson loved her aunt, too—not in the same way she loved Alec, of course, but Carson was willing to sacrifice even one of her precious few days with Alec if it meant restoring some measure of her aunt's happiness. "Maybe we can go to the beach and have that picnic you wanted."

"No, no, I know you're busy, too," said Jane. "You and Alec, I'm sure you both want to spend as much time together as you can."

"Well, yes, but I want to be with you, too," said Carson.

Her aunt hesitated then, and turned to Carson, but before she could give her answer, Lawrence appeared in the kitchen doorway. "Hello, Carson," he said in a flat voice.

"Oh, Lawrie, dinner's not ready yet," said Jane, blinking and turning away from Carson, plunging her hands back into the water in the sink where the lettuce leaves were soaking. "Go back to whatever important thing you were doing."

"I didn't come for food," Lawrence said. "I came for Carson."

"Me?" Carson put down the knife and looked at her uncle quizzically, but he only nodded. "You want to talk to me?"

"Yes, very much," he said.

So this was going to be it. The big scold. He'd somehow found out that his niece had actually become lovers with Alec Breve, and he was going to insist on breaking it up. He was furious with her. Carson felt the muscles in her stomach tighten as she girded herself for the argument that was sure to follow, the wearisome back-and-forth volley of: *I love him madly* and *But you're too young.*

"Come into my study, Carson, all right?" Lawrence asked, and Carson nodded, wiping her hands on a cloth towel before following him out of the kitchen and across the cool red tile floor.

Carson entered her uncle's study, and he closed the door behind her with a quiet click. When he turned around to face her, she saw that his expression wasn't at all angry. In fact, it seemed more sad than anything else, and suddenly Carson was frightened.

"Please sit down," her uncle said. "There's something I need to tell you."

CHAPTER FIVE

Carson reached behind her, found the chair cushion, slowly sat down across from her uncle. Lawrence removed his glasses, folded them up, and sighed, shaking his head. "What I have to tell you," he said, "is difficult for me. But it will be much more difficult for you; I'm well aware of that, believe me."

Oh God, something has happened to one of my parents, Carson thought. A car accident, she imagined, and she closed her eyes as if to ward off the blow of terrible news.

But when Lawrence spoke again he surprised her. "It's about Alec," he said.

Alec? She had just left him in Lisbon; surely nothing could have happened to him.

"I received a telegram today," Lawrence continued. "It was from London, from the undersecretary at the Ministry of Defence. The contents of the telegram are classified. Urgently so. Yet I have been sitting here all afternoon since it arrived, trying my damned best to figure out how to handle what is clearly a very delicate and pressing situation. And I've decided, Carson, that there's really no way to keep you in the dark. That, in fact, it's essential that you *not* be kept in the dark."

"I don't understand," Carson interrupted. "What are you telling me?"

"I'm telling you," Lawrence began, "that your Alec Breve is not who you think he is. That he's not simply a hardworking young academic physicist on the side of God and the Queen." Lawrence's voice was sour as he spoke. "That in fact he's a member of a pro-Fascist group that calls itself the Watchers. That he is sharing his expanding store of highly technical information with young German scientists who are essentially his counterparts."

All Carson could do was laugh. Her laughter came out louder than she'd thought. "This is the craziest thing I've ever heard," she said. "Your information is completely wrong. It's so wrong it's insane," she went on. "I mean, Alec is concerned about the situation in Germany the way his friends are. I've heard him speak about it. But how could he have 'highly technical' information that would be useful? He studies *heat*."

But Lawerence shook his head. "No," he said. "I'm afraid it's not that simple, Carson. Alec also studied radio waves when he was at Cambridge. He was a top student in those classes. We have suspicions that he is instructing the Germans in technologies for intercepting British telegraphic codes. And should there be another war . . ."

His voice faltered here, and then he shifted in his chair, his tone softening just slightly. He looked up at her, and then down at the letter opener on his blotter. He pushed it one way across the felt fabric, then another.

"Look, Carson, I do know this is tough for you. But it's true. We know Alec is involved with the Watchers. We have proof."

"What proof?" she said.

Her uncle opened his mouth, then shook his head. "I can't say," he finally answered her. "It would be a breach of security. Already I've had to go through extraordinary channels just to be able to divulge what little I've already told you. Ever since I received the cable this afternoon, I've been on the telephone to Whitehall securing clearance for you to know even this much." He glanced up at her, and for a moment she actually felt sorry for him. Clearly this conversation was taking a toll on her uncle. His eyes were sorrowful, as if asking his niece for forgiveness.

"Maybe there's been a mistake," she said. "Some horrible misunderstanding."

But already her uncle was shaking his head. "I'm afraid not, Carson. The evidence is, shall I say, compelling." He looked her in the eye. "It's *him.*"

"Whatever happened to innocent until proven guilty?"

"Yes, well"—he cleared his throat—"this isn't a court of law, and I'm afraid that sometimes legal niceties are among the first victims of war."

"But there is no war."

"Don't kid yourself, Carson. This is very grave business, and these are very grave times. It's one thing to be pro-Fascist, a follower of Sir Oswald Mosley and his Blackshirt crowd. And you're right, you can't convict someone for what's in his heart. People are allowed to meet and discuss political convictions, no matter how heinous they are to us. But when that person takes his sympathies and uses them to provide *classified information* to a country whose leadership is heading in an alarming direction—well, that's another matter entirely. Although on the surface I've tried to appear calm about the news that's coming out of Germany—the brutality of the Nazi party, the anti-immigration stance, the condoned violence toward Jews—in fact my colleagues and I are increasingly convinced that war is inevitable."

He sighed deeply and shook his head. He glanced up at Carson, then back at the letter opener. He picked it up and absently ran a fingertip along the long golden wedge. "What does it take," he asked, "to remind people that war is a nightmare from which recovery takes generations? Apparently, collective amnesia is in fashion. And people like your friend Alec are part of this. They feel that Germany has some good ideas. They think they have more in common with the German elite than the British lorry drivers. Some of them may loathe Hitler personally, but they also think, sometimes for ideological reasons, and other times purely for economic ones, that brokering a deal with the German party in power isn't such a bad thing for Britain. So they hold their noses and do it. Damn!"

He'd drawn blood. Lawrence dropped the letter opener to the desk blotter and examined the tip of his forefinger. A pin drop of red pooled there. Carson leaned forward in her chair and made a sympathetic sound, but Lawrence shook his head fiercely and stuck the fingertip to his lips. Somehow Carson knew that her uncle would disapprove of any offer of help now, as if her wanting to attend to a matter as minor as a flesh wound would have communicated to him that she didn't understand the importance of this conversation. So she sat back in her chair and tried to match his level of solemnity.

"For what it's worth," Carson said, "I've never heard Alec

utter one word that you might consider elitist, or anti-immigration, or anything else one of these Watchers would say. Really, if you knew Alec, really knew him the way I do, you'd see. He *isn't* very political."

"Oh, please," Lawrence snapped, "everyone's political. To live in the world is to be political. If you think you're exempt from it because you're young, or 'not interested,' or not educated in the matter, well, you're sadly mistaken. Alec Breve is 'interested' in politics, very much so, and so should you be. Just because Philippa has chosen to raise you in such a sheltered manner doesn't mean she can actually shelter you."

Carson opened her mouth to speak, perhaps to defend her mother's choices, but her uncle overrode her.

"Nor *should* she shelter you," he said with emphasis. "Please forgive me for speaking harshly of Phil—" He caught himself, and softened his tone. "For speaking harshly of your mother. But these convictions of mine transcend family niceties now." He looked up from his finger and met Carson's eyes. "You've come over here this summer, Carson, in order to see a little bit of the world. Perhaps you're seeing more of it than you bargained for. But that can't be helped. In fact, it's to be celebrated, don't you think?"

Carson didn't move. Neither did her uncle. The two of them simply sat there in the stifling heat of a summer afternoon in a villa in Portugal, and let the moment breathe.

Carson breathed. She felt herself breathe. She felt herself run the palm of her hand along the white cotton fabric that separated the outside world from the skin of her flat stomach, felt herself rub there, in a circle, as if to calm herself, to keep herself from breathing too hard, or from feeling too much.

She would have to choose. She had wanted the freedom to make her own choices in life, and now she had that freedom, and with it a choice beyond imagining. To one side was her uncle, spouting what seemed to her perfect nonsense. To the other was her lover, professing his undying devotion. And in the middle was Carson, and the hell of it was that even though she was trying to compose herself and remain calm and tell herself that there must be a reasonable explanation for whatever it was some anonymous operative in British intelligence had supposedly discovered and passed along to her uncle, she could nonetheless feel even now a stab of uncertainty about Alec, a wedge of doubt widening inside her, as if her uncle's letter opener had pricked not his finger but her heart.

Yes, she knew Alec, knew him as well as she'd ever known anyone. Of that, she was sure. But, she had to ask herself, precisely how well *was* that? How well could anyone ever know someone else—*really* know, *truly* see into, the soul of another? Wasn't it, after all, difficult enough to know oneself? Wasn't this the lesson that Carson had been learning all summer, over and over again, ever since that afternoon on the aft deck of the *Queen Mary* when she'd decided that she wasn't the adventurous type after all? Wasn't that resolutely nonadventuring virginal homebody now an experienced woman with a lover who might be an international spy?

Carson almost laughed. But that would have been disrespectful of her uncle, disastrously so. What she wished she could do was to plead innocence—to confess a literal lack of experience. "Experienced" she might be, as the American euphemism went, but knowledgeable, and wise, and able to draw from the well of worldly endeavors, she most decidedly was not.

"Well," she began, "if Alec really is a Fascist, as you say, then he's been able to successfully fool all his friends. You should hear them talk; they trust one another, they know one another intimately. They would be just as shocked by this news as I am."

Her uncle, she could see from his overly earnest expression, was paying her the courtesy of a hearing. But that's *just* what he was paying her: a courtesy. *Don't patronize me,* he'd once snapped at his wife within Carson's earshot, in a momentary departure from their usual cheerful banter; even so, that's precisely what he was doing now to Carson. He was patronizing her, merely hearing her out, letting her expend her girlish exertions until, at last, she would come around to his inarguably airtight compendium of facts relating to the subject of one Alec Breve. *No, no, do go on—this is fascinating!* she could almost hear him say, even as he sighed inwardly.

What, she wondered, could she possibly do to show him she meant what she said—or, at the very least, to show him she deserved his respect?

And then she knew.

"What," she said to her uncle, "do *you* think I should do?"

Uncle Lawrence raised his eyebrows. He'd probably been trained *not* to raise his eyebrows in a situation such as this, but there they were: eyebrows, up.

"Well," he said, taking a deep breath, drawing back in his chair, his gaze raking the desktop, "well, he's not to know we're on to him." Then her uncle caught himself. He glanced up at Carson, and he leaned forward, placing his hands firmly on the blotter, splaying the fingertips. "Are you absolutely quite sure you're on board?"

"Oh, Uncle Lawrence," she said, "I'm not sure of anything."

Suddenly Carson collapsed, burying her head in her hands. She pitched forward, and it was as if everything she'd kept contained inside all summer had suddenly loosed itself. She pressed her forehead into her cool knees, knew somewhere in the back of her mind that her uncle would interpret this display as some sort of sign of weakness, and decided she didn't care. She heard her uncle give a guttural curse, and she heard the distant scraping of a chair, and then, after a moment, she felt his hands on her shoulders. She wished she could be stronger. She had so much *wanted* to be stronger. She had wanted to be strong, and simple, and uncomplicated. Uncomplicated, where she came from, was a virtue. But then, she had wanted Alec Breve to be uncomplicated, too. She had wished him to be a simple physicist who would follow her to the States. And maybe that's what he was, in fact. Or, maybe not. And it was in that shadowy realm of maybe/maybe-not that her uncle was now forcing her to dwell.

"None of us is," she heard her uncle saying softly, gently, as he rubbed her shoulders. "Sure of anything, I mean. It just takes some of us longer to learn that lesson than others. And some never learn. You're fortunate, Carson. You're learning it at an early age."

"I don't feel very fortunate," she said.

"No, I don't suppose you would," her uncle said, releasing her shoulders.

Carson sat up. She wiped the back of her hand against her eyes. She smoothed her skirt. She nodded her head, indicating that she would be all right now.

"It's just so much to take in all at once," she said. "I mean, it all just seems so incredible. That you should receive an urgent cable involving the very man I've happened to fall in love with."

Her uncle didn't answer at first. After a moment, he came out from behind her chair and went back behind his desk. But he didn't sit. Instead, when he began speaking again, he was facing away from her, staring out the window.

"Yes, well, it's not quite a coincidence," he said. "It turns out that he's why I'm here. Why you're here, and Jane. It isn't a coincidence that I chose a house to summer in just down the road, so to speak, from the most important physics conference of the year."

"What?" Carson said.

"We've known for some time that someone at Cambridge has been getting military secrets to the Germans. We just haven't known who." He turned back toward Carson, and the matter-of-factness in the tone of what he said next made Carson shiver. "Now we do."

Carson could feel the sting of the tears welling up in her throat again. "And yet you let me fall in love with him, knowing who he might be?"

Her uncle's shoulders sagged. "Carson, there are twenty-three representatives from Cambridge at this conference. Your Alec is—what is the American expression?—low man on the totem pole. He seemed an unlikely candidate for a mole. I can't say I was particularly pleased that you'd gotten involved with someone from Cambridge, but then I thought back to that first night at dinner, on the train, and I have to say that Alec had struck me as harmless enough." Her uncle gave a small, unhappy laugh. "I must be getting too old for this job."

Carson tried to summon a response, but nothing came to her. She realized that it almost didn't matter if what her uncle was saying was true, if Alec was in fact a member of the Watchers or any of those other awful things that Lawrence had said he was. What mattered was that she could never trust Alec again.

Trust. All summer long Carson had been learning to trust herself—to trust not the judgment of her mother, or her aunt and uncle, but herself. To make up her own mind. And she had. She had trusted herself to trust Alec. And where had it gotten her? For her, she knew now, there could be no going back, no returning to the state of innocence she'd inhabited when she entered her uncle's study. Or, rather, she *would* be going back: back to Paris, back to the ship, and then back to Connecticut, where she would fall into her mother's arms, weeping. *Back where I belong,* Carson thought bitterly.

"So that's it, then," she finally said in a dull, numb voice. "You arrest Alec, I never see him again, and life goes on."

"Not quite."

She looked up at her uncle. He went back to his chair now, opened a small wooden box on his desk, took out a cigarette, and lit it.

"Now that we're on to his game, Alec Breve is more valuable to us as a free man than as a prisoner. We have good reason to believe the Watchers are conspiring with certain

German officials to put an entire network of information in place before the advent of a war. And that," Lawrence said, loosing a plume of smoke from the side of his mouth, "is where you come in."

"What do you mean?"

"Alec mustn't know we're on to him. It's absolutely imperative that nothing change. We don't want to scare him off. If the niece of a man he knows to be in British intelligence should suddenly give him the cold shoulder—well, the consequences could be catastrophic."

"So what do you want me to do?" Carson said. "Continue seeing him?"

"Precisely."

Carson simply stared back at her uncle, uncomprehendingly.

"Look, Carson," he went on, "I haven't been telling you all this simply to let you down easily. I haven't been working all afternoon to get security clearance for my niece just so I could protect her from the likes of Alec Breve. Of course I appreciate how hurt you've been by what I've told you today. But this is far bigger than a love story between two young people. For your own sake as well as the country's, I've needed to get you involved."

"So," she said, "you want me to keep seeing Alec so that I can . . . keep tabs on him?" she said. "So that I can report what I've learned to you?"

Uncle Lawrence nodded. "That's exactly what I'm saying," he said.

"Then I would be a spy," she said.

"Yes, in a manner of speaking," said Uncle Lawrence. "A spy for Britain. Look, I wouldn't ask you to do this if I thought

I'd be placing you in any danger. Nor would I ask you if I didn't believe that the situation was of the utmost importance. And I certainly wouldn't ask you if I didn't think you could handle it."

He waited a moment for this to sink in. Carson wasn't sure whether she should be flattered or angered—angered that her uncle thought he could win her favor through flattery.

"You've impressed me a great deal this summer, Carson. What I had imagined was a girl who had grown up extremely sheltered and protected by her lifestyle. Philippa herself grew up that way, too, as did Jane. But Jane didn't want any part of it, finally, and for some reason it took falling in love with me for her to see that. You came around to the conclusion the same way, I suspect. By falling in love with Alec Breve."

"And now you want me to use that love to betray him?"

"I want you to use that love, if that's indeed what it is, to stop Alec from betraying Britain. Look," her uncle went on, lowering his eyes, "it's none of my business, and I don't mean this to sound uncaring, because it's not. I care for you deeply. But it's entirely possible that Alec's declarations of affection for you are motivated by his knowledge that you're the niece of a member of British intelligence."

"You think he's using me to get to you?" Carson said.

"I don't know what to think. All I know for absolutely certain is that you mustn't alter your behavior in any way that would raise his suspicions, and if you happen to find out something that might pertain to the war effort, by all means let me know. I'm terribly sorry, Carson, but getting you involved in this is unavoidable. Still, it's only for three more days," he added.

Carson closed her eyes. Three more days. Until the moment she walked into this room, she had been trying to figure out a way to make her three days left in Lisbon last a lifetime. Now she couldn't wait for them to be over.

"You realize," she heard her uncle say, "that no one else knows about this. Not even your aunt Jane."

Carson opened her eyes. "You haven't told Jane?"

"No," said Lawrence. "The kind of work I'm in—well, we try not to make exceptions. Of course my wife is entirely trustworthy. You and I both know that. But the Home Office doesn't. And it isn't up to me to use my judgment as I see fit. If everyone were allowed such leeway, it would be a poor policy indeed. No, Jane knows nothing of this, nor should she."

"So what does Jane think we're talking about in here?" Carson asked. "Won't she think it strange that you called me into your study?"

Lawrence nodded. "I've worked that out. Here's how it will be: We're going to pretend that I asked you to stop seeing Alec, that I told you the relationship was getting far too serious. And that you flat-out refused to obey me."

"You want me to lie to Jane?"

"Exactly," said her uncle. "In about a minute, you and I are going to deliberately raise our voices, turning this conversation into something that will sound like a heated argument. And then, if I know her, your aunt is most likely going to come to the door of this room, fling it open, and demand that we stop. She'll calm both of us down, because she's good at that, and she'll think that she's talked reason into us. Then you'll go on seeing Alec, and I'll apologize and say that I was being unreasonable, or something like that. Do you follow me?"

"Yes," said Carson quietly. And then, as if she'd been re-hearsing this for weeks, she suddenly raised her voice to him and said the first words that came to mind: "I don't care what you think, Lawrence! I don't care what you say about Alec! I love him! *I love him!*"

There was a beat, during which her uncle looked at her as if he believed what she was saying—or at least believed that she believed it. Then he blinked, nodded to her, and matched her tone. "Not if you know what's good for you!"

In a matter of seconds, Carson could hear hurried female footsteps across the tile floor elsewhere in the house, and the next thing she knew, the door to the study swung open, just as her uncle had predicted.

The beginning of Lawrence's plans went off without a hitch. Aunt Jane was given a chance to broker peace that evening between her husband and niece, and she did so swiftly and calmly. Carson felt the burden of having to lie to her aunt, but when she excused herself after dinner, saying she didn't feel well and needed to go to bed, she was telling the truth. She was sick with exhaustion, if nothing else. Carson crept under the sheets while the last of the long day's sun was still stretching across the red tile floor of her room. As she lay there, she didn't even try to make sense of the day's events. Instead, she pictured herself in Alec's bed, saw his arms wrap-ping around her tightly, and, just before drifting into the deep sleep of emotional fatigue, realized that as much as her life had changed when she'd met Alec Breve, tonight it had changed yet again.

The following morning, Alec, Freddy, Michael, and Tom

arrived in the open-topped jalopy they'd rented for a trip to the beach. The car pulled up to the villa in a cloud of dust, the rubber horn bleating cheerful, wheezy hellos. In the front hall of the villa, Carson stood very still, looking through the window at the sight of Alec behind the wheel. He had an old moth-eaten sweater on, and his hair had been blown about in the wind during the drive from Lisbon. He looked happy and carefree. As far as he knew, this was a day like any other—a day to go to the beach with his girlfriend and three of his best pals.

Alec hopped out of the car and headed up the stone path to the Villa do Giraldo, past the shrubbery and red and gold flowers that grew wildly, and past the low-slung bees circling their blooms. Aunt Jane let him into the villa, and Carson heard the two of them make idle conversation.

"Did you have a good trip?" Jane asked.

"Oh, yes, thanks, Mrs. Emmett," Alec said. "The jalopy held up well, considering the state of Portuguese roads."

"Well, Carson's right inside. I think she's fixed you all a pretty nice lunch."

Carson had, in fact, spent the morning deviling eggs and making a salad, but she had barely paid attention to what she was doing; instead, she had observed her hands shredding lettuce and mashing egg yolks as though they were someone else's hands, not her own. She felt as though she had gone outside her own body and was no longer inhabiting it. This body, which Alec had touched and caressed, was now an empty husk. Numb. That was the word for what she felt, and the sensation—or lack of it—stayed with her as she went to meet Alec and let him kiss her cheek and embrace her lightly.

It stayed with her as she sat beside him, in the front seat of the car, on the road to Cascais, and it stayed all day at the beach as they lay on the sand, or swam together in the pale, shimmering water.

She hadn't known how she would respond to the sight of him, and so she had allowed herself to be drained of desire, of all physical anticipation. She no longer had any idea who Alec was; she didn't even know how to think about the situation—about this man who could appear sensitive and caring yet harbor deep prejudices and hatreds. Yet, when she saw him waving from the jalopy as it pulled up to the Villa do Giraldo, when she felt the weight of his arm around her shoulders during the drive to the beach, or now, as she surveyed his long, tanned limbs emerging, dripping, from the sea, she experienced a vague version of the stirring that always accompanied the sight of him, or his touch. It was something basic, something primal; it couldn't be helped. But Carson also felt a new sensation: revulsion—toward Alec, certainly, but also toward what her uncle was asking of her. Lawrence, Carson realized now, had no idea of just what his plan would require her to do. He'd never have asked her—never have hatched this plan for her to remain with Alec—if he'd known how far the romance between the two of them had progressed, and what acts of intimacy it involved.

"Darling?" Alec said.

Carson started. She had settled herself on a blanket on the sand, and now Alec was dropping himself beside her. She shaded her eyes and looked at him. A playful if cautious face looked back.

"Is there anything wrong?" he said.

She smiled weakly at him and pushed herself up on one elbow.

"I'm fine," she said. "Just a bad night's sleep."

Well, at least that wasn't entirely a lie. She *had* woken several times in a state of agitation, feeling sure she'd been having a nightmare, but she could never remember what it was. And then she would remember that the real nightmare was what she'd be facing in the morning—the bad dream she was living right now.

"You're quite sure?" he pressed.

"Of course I'm sure."

Freddy Hunt was sitting beside them on the blanket on the sand, and overheard the conversation. "Alec, don't you know anything about women?" he said jokingly. "They're extremely fickle. One minute they love you, the next minute they're as cold as ice."

"Stop," murmured Carson. "I'm not being remotely cold. Alec is making it up."

"Alec is always making things up," said Freddy. "The man lives in his head, can't you see that? You get a little deluded when all you do is cogitate all day. Thank God you came along, Carson, to show him that there's more to life than a thermodynamic equation written on a blackboard."

The idle talk was unnerving her. She lay back against the blanket, her head resting against the rough local wool, and closed her eyes. The strong Cascais sun beat down on her, but she didn't care. In the distance she heard Alec's voice. He was saying something to his friends about being worried about Carson. "She's not herself," she heard him murmur. That was true. *But neither are you, Alec Breve*, she thought.

Next thing she knew, Carson heard a soft moaning. She opened her eyes to see who it was, and realized that *she* was the person moaning. Above her was a circle of concerned faces: Alec, Freddy, Tom, Michael, and a few strangers, blocking out the blazing sun. *The sun.* That was why she was moaning. She had fallen asleep in the sun and gotten burned. When she opened her mouth to speak, her lips were parched.

Alec knelt down beside her. "Carson, look, you've gotten a bit of a burn, it seems. I hadn't realized you were so sensitive to the sun. We need to get you home."

Connecticut, Carson thought at first, then realized that he meant Sintra. But she was right the first time. Going now to her aunt and uncle's house would simply be a temporary measure, but Carson felt so sick from the sun that she let Alec help her up from the blanket, and she leaned against him as they went back to the car. He carefully covered her with the blanket. "So you don't get a chill in the wind as we drive," he said, and she surrendered to his tenderness, leaning into him and closing her eyes and, for the rest of the ride, drawing as much human comfort from his touch as she could.

When they arrived back at the villa, Alec carried Carson inside while Jane and Lawrence hovered over, exclaiming in upset voices.

"Brew some tea, Mrs. Emmett, would you please?" Alec asked. "And then if you could put it in a large bowl with plenty of ice. The tannic acid in the tea is a good salve for sunburns. I know that from personal experience."

So Carson lay on her bed and let her aunt apply poultices of the iced tea. Alec was right; she did start to feel better. Though nothing could be done to take away the sunburn itself, at least the effects of it wouldn't be so severe. Aunt Jane gave Carson two grains of aspirin and some cold *limonata* to drink. By now, Alec, Freddy, Michael, and Tom had quietly left and driven back to the city, and Carson was alone in her bedroom with her aunt. Evening was just falling; off in the kitchen of the villa, Lawrence was cutting up a chicken for dinner.

"What happened today, Carson?" Aunt Jane asked as she sat on the edge of Carson's bed, beneath the mosquito netting.

"Alec told you," said Carson flatly. "I lay in the sun too long and got burned."

"No, he said you seemed peculiar *before* that," said Jane. "That you seemed upset, for reasons he couldn't explain. That you were almost unfriendly to him. Of course, I didn't say a word about the argument you had last night with Lawrie, but that's what this is about, isn't it?"

"Yes," said Carson vaguely.

"I thought as much."

Carson sat up in bed, leaning her head heavily against the muslin pillow sham. "Aunt Jane," she asked with sudden emotion in her voice, "do you think it's really possible for a person to know what's inside another person? Inside their heart?"

Her aunt appraised her in the dim light of the bedroom. "Well, it depends on what you mean by that," she said. "Two people in love—they like to think that they're twins, in a way. That they've spent their whole life until now wandering the earth without their other half. And now they've found it, and it's a great relief. Usually, people who have recently fallen in love want to tell each other everything, want to pour out

99

the contents of their heart." She paused. "Is that what you're getting at?"

"In a way," said Carson. She wanted to tell her aunt what Lawrence had said to her in his study the night before, but she knew it was essential that she not do that. In fact, Carson had already begun doing exactly what her uncle asked her *not* to do: she'd behaved differently toward Alec. She'd been distant to him, she'd withdrawn her affections. He was beginning to ask questions, to wonder what's really going on here— precisely what her uncle had instructed Carson not to let happen under any circumstances.

I'm a terrible spy, she thought as she sat there on the bed with her aunt. *I've really got to do much better than this.*

Later that night, when the aspirin had taken effect along with the iced-tea poultices, Carson managed to eat a little of the roast chicken that Lawrence had sweetly if clumsily prepared. After the meal, during which no one spoke very much, she asked her aunt and uncle if she might use the telephone. Of course, they said, and so Carson sat in the living room speaking into the heavy receiver.

"*Fala ingles?*" she asked the operator.

"*Sim,*" said the woman across the crackling line.

Then Carson asked in English whether she could place a call to Lisboa, to the Pensão Moderna, *por favor.*

When Alec got on the line, he sounded so relieved to hear her voice that his own voice came out in a rush of air. "Carson," he said, "oh, you're all right?"

"I was stupid to have lain on that blanket like that," she said. "Once, back in Connecticut, I got a terrible burn. I'd forgotten how susceptible I am."

"So you haven't turned into a piece of fried *bacalhau?*" he asked, and she pretended to laugh as she told him that no, she hadn't.

"There's something else I wanted to say," she said to him.

"Yes, what is it?" he asked.

"You remember today, how you thought I was acting strangely?"

"Of course I do," he said.

"Well, you were right. I was."

"Finally! The girl admits it! I knew I wasn't going crazy," said Alec.

"I was feeling confused," she found herself saying. "Things have happened so quickly this summer. Time has been compressed for me; it's as though you and I have been together for years, and yet of course it's only weeks." It amazed her how fluidly and easily the lies came. She almost believed them herself—that the reason for her strangeness today was the headiness of love. "But I want to see you as soon as I can," Carson said. "To reassure you that it was only a momentary lapse. Because"—and she paused here, experiencing, despite herself, a secret thrill at still being able to say these words, as if even now they contained the same illicit heat they'd held for her all summer, as if by saying them she might somehow erase all the horrible knowledge she'd gained in the past day and return to a time when they were true—"I love you, Alec."

And so it was that the very next day Carson Weatherell found herself back in the center of Lisbon with Alec Breve, the two of them walking along broad, leafy avenues the way they had done before Uncle Lawrence's pronouncement. She'd had nothing to report to her uncle regarding the previous day, of course, yet her uncle had insisted that she tell him everything. "You never know what might prove important later on," he said, sitting behind the desk in his study that morning, scrupulously copying down Carson's description of the drive to the beach and what little she remembered of the beach itself. She supposed she would have to perform the same duty the following morning, though the evening, as it passed, seemed as unpromising as the beach: a beefsteak dinner in a tiny, narrow restaurant lit by long, dripping tapers, followed, Alec informed her as the meal drew to a close and the waiters began clearing a space at the very back of the restaurant for a small platform and a microphone, by a show.

"*Fado*," Alec said.

"*Fado?* What's that?"

"You'll see," he said.

Within moments a young, beautiful man appeared on the platform holding a guitar. He wore a simple white cotton shirt with embroidery; it was opened down his chest, revealing bronzed skin. His eyes were gleaming and sorrowful as he put the guitar strap around his neck and began to sing. He was a *fadista*, she learned, a performer of the old Portuguese art of *fado*, an expressive tradition that for centuries had combined tales of lost love and forgotten glory with music. The combination was wrenching. All she could think of as she watched and listened was how everything had been destroyed between herself and Alec. The only difference between herself and the *fadista* was that though her feelings of love for her lover were dying, the object of her love was still close at hand.

Later that evening, in Alec's room at the *pensão*, she made love with him again, and not only because if she didn't, then she knew he would surely grow suspicious. After all, she could have used the sunburn as an excuse. And maybe, she thought, some part of her had wanted to stay in the sun too long yesterday, to spare her having to face a moment just like this.

But that was yesterday. Pressing her sunburned body now against Alec's, she felt the surface of his muscles and the tension collected within, waiting to spring. She thought of the Alec of old, the friend and lover in whose presence she prayed for time to stop. She thought of her uncle, and how she would leave this part of the evening out of her morning report. She thought of the young *fadista* onstage tonight, and how palpable his sense of isolation and loss was. As Alec pressed urgently against her, covering her neck, her collarbone, her mouth with kisses, Carson realized that tears were streaming from her eyes. At first she thought she was crying for the *fadista*, but then she realized that she was crying, of course, only for herself.

CHAPTER SIX

Two days later, Carson and Alec traveled back to Paris on the same train that had brought them to Lisbon. Then, as now, they were not officially together. Carson, of course, was still in the care of her aunt and uncle, and Alec was still bunking with his three Cambridge mates, but Carson couldn't help thinking that what might have seemed to Alec like a temporary exercise in discretion—in keeping up appearances—was in fact, without his knowledge, final: a farewell.

And one that was beginning to take its toll on Carson. For the past three days in Portugal she had been willing to act the role of devoted lover—a part, she had to admit, that she had grown willing to play. And she'd apparently played it well. After that first semidisastrous day on the beach, Alec would have had no reason to suspect anything. The following day he had seen Carson for dinner and the *fado* show and a round of lovemaking back at the *pensão,* and then he had seen her again the day after that, their last together in Portugal.

They had planned to spend the day exploring the coast. Alec had told Carson he'd heard of yet one more noble, crumbled *castelo* in Sintra that looked down on the coastline, where the waves, no doubt, would gently be striking the rocks. But when Carson had arrived at Alec's door at the Pensão Moderna, the thought of sightseeing had struck them both as absurd. The only sights they wanted to see on this day—the only landscapes they wished to commit to memory—were their own.

And so they did, beginning at noon, stretching through siesta, and then lasting eventually into the evening. Sometimes during that final, endless afternoon, Carson would find herself thinking about what she was supposed to be doing here—what her uncle and England expected of her. Once, in an attempt to draw Alec out, Carson offered this: "He expects war, you know."

Alec, lying on his back, trying to catch his breath, waited a beat. Then he said, "Who?"

"My uncle."

"Your uncle. He expects war, does he?" Alec's tone suggested not so much curiosity as bafflement.

"You asked what he thought once, remember?"

"Did I?"

"And he's not alone," Carson went on. "He tells me the entire Ministry of Defence considers war absolutely inevitable."

"Well," Alec said, sitting up and turning toward Carson, his arms encircling her as if to devour her, "do you know what I consider inevitable?" And then he pulled Carson on top of him.

Wherefore art thou? she'd once wondered about Alec, meaning: Who are you? Now she could ask the same question of herself. Who was this woman who slipped so easily between the role of lover and betrayer? Who found it astonishingly easy to lead a double life? Who routinely did things that until recently she would have considered unimaginable, and unforgivable? She lied to Jane. She lied to Alec. She snooped, rooting through his private things. That final afternoon with Alec, while he was down the hall in the washroom, Carson climbed out of bed and furtively shuffled through the stack of mail lying on his bureau. But it, too, was unrevealing; there were innocuous-seeming letters from friends back at Cambridge, and a note from the wealthy dowager, Mrs. Bertram, who had employed Alec's mother as a housekeeper when he was growing up, and who, after his mother's death, had assumed the role of second mother to Alec. Once Mrs. Bertram had seemed to be as much a part of Carson and Alec's future together as had her own parents. Alec often talked of how one day he would lead Carson down the quiet streets of Bloomsbury, past the British Museum, to the house where Mrs. Bertram still kept a room for Alec, just as Carson tempted him with visions of the Weatherell family's glassed-in porch, its view of the sun falling gently on the snow-covered lawn, a table set for an American version of "tea." Carson sighed deeply now, slipped the letter back into its envelope, and gently returned it to the top of the bureau, where it rejoined the pile of letters and a fountain pen and a hairbrush and all the other minutiae of what once had been, and soon would be again, Alec Breve's life without Carson Weatherell.

Just as he had that first night on the train, Alec joined Carson and Jane and Lawrence for dinner on the ride back to Paris. The meal passed innocuously, with much talk of Sintra and no talk of war, and at the earliest opportunity that she could do so without raising suspicions, Carson retired to her compartment. She changed into her nightclothes and climbed up the metal ladder to the bunk that a porter had turned down. Carson lay there awake for a long time, trying to lose herself in the rhythm of the train, and staring at the ceiling. Somewhere along the corridor slept Alec. Carson could picture him lying on his back, his tanned chest bare, smoking a cigarette and thinking about . . . what? About her? About the Watchers? About Germany and military secrets and the glories of Nazism?

"No," she said aloud, surprising herself.

"Pardon?" The voice of her aunt came from the bunk below. Carson had long before turned off her reading lamp, but she could see from the spill of light on the red carpet that her aunt was still awake.

"Nothing," said Carson. "I must have been dozing off."

Carson heard the dull thump of a book closing and then the shifting of sheets. After a moment, her aunt's light went out. But then Jane spoke again.

"Carson," she said, "is there anything you'd like to talk about?"

"No. But thank you. Good night."

Another silence. Then: "Sometimes, Carson, and I do hope you don't take this the wrong way, but sometimes I wish you could really talk to me. Oh, I don't mean the way we do. We get along famously already, don't you think? And I've had a marvelous time getting to know you better this summer, and the fact is, I do feel I really know you now. You're not this invisible niece I rarely see. You're flesh and blood now. Family.

So: mission accomplished. That's what I hoped would happen when I invited you to spend the summer with Lawrie and me, and it did happen. I do think we'll have a friendship now. But," she went on, "there are times—and maybe I'm being presumptuous even to suggest this, and maybe I've no right to say this, none at all—but sometimes, Carson, I wish you could open up to me a bit more. I would like very much if you came to feel that you could confide in me the way . . . well, the way a daughter would with her mother."

Carson didn't answer at first. The fact was, she wished it, too. Her aunt was kind, and worldly, and wise. Carson felt if she could confide in Jane, unburden herself to her, that her aunt would know what to tell her, how to make her feel better. And she was sure, in turn, that this sharing of secrets would make her aunt feel better. Poor Jane, Carson thought now, married to a husband who was married to the Home Office. Jane loved Lawrie, of course; but that love came at a cost. Maybe all love did. After the initial explosion of passion, when the all-consuming part of the romance has passed and the outside world has begun to bleed through, like the morning light through bedroom blinds, you start to find out who the other person really is, and he or she finds out more about you, and then you decide whether it's worth the cost. For Jane, the kindnesses and comforts of Lawrie outweighed his devotion to his job. But what could outweigh a lover's secret devotion to fascism? Nothing.

Carson, though, had given her word to Lawrence—to Britain and to liberty. She couldn't speak to anyone about what had happened to her these past three days—no, not even to her mother when Carson got back in Connecticut, let alone to an aunt, however close and wise. And so Carson shook her head in the dark, bit her lip, and forced herself to answer, "Yes, Jane. I'd like that, too. I feel the same way about you, if it's any help. And if I had anything to talk about, you'd be the first to hear it, I swear."

"I'm glad you said that," Jane answered after a moment.

So am I, thought Carson. And then, as the train whistle shrilled mournfully, she fell asleep.

On the ship home to the States, this time traveling without the chaperone her parents had hired for the voyage over, Carson spent a good deal of time standing on deck and smoking, looking out at the water. Her mother and father would be shocked to see her with a cigarette in hand, but then again, they'd be shocked by plenty of things that had happened to her over the course of the summer. All they'd wanted was for her to go on a debutante's tour of Europe; they'd meant for her to see the Tower of London and the Eiffel Tower, which she had done, and then to see some places more obscure and quaint, such as a coastal town in Portugal, which she'd also done. But they'd never meant for her to fall in love, and certainly not with someone like Alec Breve.

She and Alec had said their good-byes. When they stepped off the Lisbon train into the dusty, windowed light of the Gare St. Lazare, Alec walked beside Carson, his arm looped through hers, and she smiled at him periodically, as she knew she ought to do. From the crowded docks of nearby Calais, it was a short boat trip across the Channel to Southampton and the *Queen Mary*, where Alec accompanied her to the dock to see her ship sail. When Jane and Lawrence tactfully disappeared to give them a few minutes alone, Alec had pulled Carson over behind the shelter of an enormous mountain of trunks and valises that were being loaded onto the ship. There he told her again that he loved her, and she saw the slightest glaze of tears in his eyes.

"I love you, too," she'd said, and then they'd kissed one final time. He smelled like leather and salt and something sweet: toffee, perhaps. It was *his* smell, something male and personal and singular, and one, Carson thought as she finally pulled away from him, that she would never smell again.

And that was it. "Mission accomplished," as her aunt had said about Carson's visit to the Continent. Minutes later, gripping the railing of the swaying metal gangplank that spanned the space between dock and ship, and receiving the calls of "bon voyage" from all her friends onshore—Jane and Alec, of course, but Freddy and Michael and Tom, too—Carson leaned over as if to give her uncle a kiss good-bye. Instead, she'd whispered into his ear, "I'm done."

Lawrence had acknowledged this last communiqué. He'd straightened, giving Carson a piercing, questioning look, and then he'd averted his glance, if not out of professional probity, then out of personal guilt. But he'd somehow managed to offer a nod of his head, too, in a manner that would have been imperceptible to anyone in the group of well-wishers who might be observing the moment closely, but meaningful to the one person who mattered most, Carson.

So, Lawrence agreed: she was, indeed, done. "Three more days," Lawrence had promised during the discussion in his office, and now those three days were up. Now Carson could hardly be much help to Lawrence, England, the democratic tradition, or anything or anyone but herself. Now Carson needed to try to get past everything that had happened this summer. To forget, and to move on. Alec would write to her, but she would not return his letters. And he would call her, too, she knew, but she would not speak to him. Eventually she would write him a farewell letter, and that would be the end of it. He wouldn't know what hit him, and if he for some reason suspected that her uncle had something to do with it—that British intelligence was on to him—well, that would be Lawrence's problem. Alec would have his problems, Lawrence would have his, and thousands of miles away, Carson would have hers.

Now, standing at the railing of a ship churning toward America, Carson took a long drag on the cigarette, then exhaled, watching the stream of smoke pour out into the open deck air. She could go through the motions of nodding hello to strolling couples on deck, of making pleasant talk with her fellow passengers at meals, of sipping a glass of champagne while listening to the band in the ballroom. She could do all that and more, if she had to. She knew that about herself now. She could do whatever she had to do until she found herself safely back on familiar ground.

Carson remembered how on the passage over to Europe she had wished to be back in her own bed as a child. That's not what she wished now. She didn't want to be a child listening to a fairy tale about a princess finding her prince. But as she flipped her cigarette toward the horizon, watching the red ember tumble toward the roiling waters below, she had to admit she wouldn't mind being back in her own bed nonetheless.

. . .

On the dock at New York Harbor a week later, Carson was received by her family as if she were a returning war hero. *If only
they knew,* she thought that night as she sat at dinner with her
parents in Connecticut and regaled them with the kinds of
touristy stories she thought they'd want to hear.

"How was Paris?" her mother asked. "Are the fashions
really as incredible as people say they are? Do women actually
walk around in those enormous hats?"

Paris. Oh, right. Vaguely, Carson recalled her time there,
and how Jane had brought her around to the various couture
houses, until she'd eaten a bad oyster and taken to bed in her
hotel. That seemed to have happened a million years earlier;
the clothes she'd bought there were folded into Carson's
steamer trunk, and they hadn't been taken out once in Portugal, for there had been no need for anything so formal.

Carson answered her mother as best she could, trying her
hardest to describe life on "the Continent," as people called
it, but being so distracted that it was obvious she was only
paying lip service to her mother's questions. Her father asked
about Germany, and how the German situation looked to Eu-
ropeans. Carson told him of the anxiety that hovered in the
air there, and what Uncle Lawrence had said about its inevitability, and her father listened well, nodding and wanting
to know more. It occurred to Carson that her father was probably surprised at how articulate she'd become about such a serious matter.

The meal—a classically American one of porterhouse
steak, mashed potatoes, an iceberg lettuce salad, and devil's

food cake, served up proudly by the Weatherell family's long-time cook, Jeannie—wound down immediately after the plates were cleared. Carson professed exhaustion, insisting she simply had to get to bed, although of course the trip back across the Atlantic had been leisurely.

And so she retreated to her own room. Here, she thought, was the one place in the world she could truly be herself. She sat on the window seat and looked out over the beautiful lawn and wondered what Alec was doing right now. She imagined him in his flat in Cambridge, for he'd once described it to her. He and his friends shared a suite of rooms that were piled high with books and teacups and writing pads. Four junior tutors at Cambridge, busy with teaching and with their own research, surely couldn't be bothered to keep things in order.

"But if you and I get married someday," Alec had said, "I promise to keep our home much better than that. I shall give up my junior-tutor ways."

"You'd better," she'd said with a laugh. It had been easy to imagine him deep in thought in his flat, a cigarette burning down to a stub between his fingers, the ashtray overflowing, his head tilted down over a book. He was a brilliant man, that much she knew. Just the way he composed his sentences let her see how intelligent he was—even if almost everything he'd said was a lie. *Especially* if almost everything he said was a lie. It took a special kind of brilliance to achieve such a seamless duplicity—a kind of brilliance, she supposed, that was not at all inconsistent with what it took to be a first-rate physicist. It was possible to be intelligent and corrupt; one had nothing to do with the other.

It was here, in the solitude of her childhood bedroom, that

Carson at last began to bend under the enormous burden of her final days in Portugal. No playacting in the Pensão Moderna now. No lies to Jane, no withholding of intimate details from Lawrence. No pretenses in train stations, no false declarations of love on docks, no forced dinner-table conversation with her parents. For ten days Carson had protected herself, had isolated herself from her emotions, steeling herself with inner resources she had no idea she possessed. She had done what she needed to do for Lawrence, for Queen, for country; for Alec, even; and then, tonight, for her parents.

Now, though, she would do what she needed to do for herself. Now, alone at last with only empty days ahead—the emptiness of days that until recently she had imagined would be full of the giddy possibilities and sober responsibilities and sense of shared adventure that come with falling in love— Carson had nobody and nothing but herself and her own thoughts. Now, in this room with its canopied bed and bookshelf full of children's classics and window seat with a view of the lawn and trees that she had gazed upon nearly every day of what once was and now was again Carson Weatherell's life without Alec Breve—now she could begin to mourn what might have been.

Slowly at first. An idle thought here: What's Alec doing now? A darker thought there: intelligence and corruption and what little they had to do with each other. And then—

And then she leaned her forehead against the leaded glass of the window. She had cried in Lawrence's office when he told her what he'd discovered about Alec, and then she had pulled herself together; and she had cried in Alec's arms the night when she found herself making love to a man she no longer knew, and she had somehow managed to compose herself on that occasion, too; and now she cried again. This time, though, Carson saw no reason to stop.

Was she wrong to have fallen in love? No. She couldn't believe that. She had *loved. She* had loved. She who had set forth at the beginning of the summer with fear and trepidation and homesickness had discovered instead the pleasure of opening herself to the unknown. And what she had found there surpassed everything she'd ever imagined—anything she'd ever thought possible, anything she could have remotely understood if she'd followed her first impulse and fled the wilds of world capitals for the safe precincts of Connecticut. For the rest of her life she would have been ignorant of the possibilities of love, and in her ignorance she wouldn't have known the difference, but now she did know the difference, and she knew she would have been the worse for not having loved.

So, rather, was she wrong to have fallen in love *with Alec Breve?*

Maybe. Maybe so. Because it wasn't just *love* she'd lost. It wasn't just love in general, love in the abstract, the love she could find described in most of the books on the shelf in her bedroom, the love she had heard about in every fairy tale her mother had ever told her. No, it was one specific love she'd lost. It was the love of Alec Breve.

Not the new Alec, the real Alec, the keeper of dark secrets, the one whose heart of hearts was forever out of reach. That person was unfathomable to Carson, though that didn't stop her from trying to figure him out. Instead it was the old Alec, the one to whom she had opened her own heart of hearts. It was the memory of that Alec that had allowed her to play her part so well during those final three days in Portugal and then on the train back to Paris, right through that last kiss and lying declaration of love on the dock at Southampton, and it was the memory of him that haunted her now. That focused her thoughts in the night, as she stared at the blank canvas of white fabric hanging above her bed. That flooded her thoughts in the morning, as soon as she opened her eyes and remembered where she was and who she was and why right this second she couldn't bear to be either. That forced her to ask herself every waking moment: *Why?*

Why couldn't it have lasted? Why did it have to end? Why couldn't Alec Breve be who she thought he was?

And the answer to all those questions, no matter how many times she asked them, no matter how many ways she found to phrase them, was always the same: because Alec Breve *wasn't* who she thought he was.

It was that simple, and that complex.

Simple, Carson told herself, pulling herself upright, pacing the length of her room, back and forth between the window seat and the edge of the bed. It was so simple. So, so, so . . . *simple,* was the only word for it. Carson balled her hand into a fist, squeezed it tight, digging her nails into her palm, as if the answer were indeed so simple, so compact, that she could actually grasp it. Alec wasn't who she thought he was; was in fact probably a monster; therefore she should be glad to be rid of him. For a moment Carson would experience a lightheadedness, as if, at last, this one insight might be just the thread she could follow to find her way back to some semblance of a normal life. *She should be glad to be rid of him.* The reasoning couldn't be clearer.

And it couldn't be less reassuring. Sinking to the bed or the window seat, she would find herself circling back again—and again and again and again and *again* and *again*—to this: She *wasn't* glad to be rid of him. It didn't matter at such moments who Alec really was. Maybe one day the fact that he wasn't who he said he was would provide some comfort. But not yet. Not now, while the wounds were still fresh—the memories of who she'd thought he was, and what she'd thought they had together, and what she'd thought the two of them together would have for the rest of their lives. Now all that mattered was that she wanted him back.

She was always traveling on that train now. She was looking through the glass of a compartment door into a smoky room and meeting the eyes of a young man as he looked up from a spray of playing cards. She was shaking the hand of that same young man minutes later at her aunt and uncle's table in the dining car. She was studying his features, admiring their asymmetry. She was hearing his voice, and laughing at his deadpan self-deprecation. She was alive to the shine of the silver in the hands of the diners in the room, the red of the roses in the vases on each table, the blinding white of the linen tablecloths.

She was more alive, and the world was more alive because of it. More real, more vibrant, more luminous. Lighter, darker; louder, closer. This was what it was like to be alive, fully alive, to be a part of the world in a way she'd never known. Sitting at the table with her aunt and uncle and Alec in the dining car, she could feel her back arch, her face flush, her fingers flex, stretch, yearn—for what? For something to hold on to. For flesh. For him.

She was walking beside him down that corridor on the train, the swaying taking them any way it wanted, so they had to hold on. To the brass railings that ran the length of the cars, yes, of course. But to each other, too. His hand on her arm. Her bare arm. The fabric ending three inches off the shoulder; his fingers below it, encircling. Encircling her flesh. Friendly. Two friends. What her aunt and uncle saw from their compartment as Carson and Alec passed: just that: two friends. Or: two friends? Future lovers? A naive niece and a possible spy, in her uncle's eye?

The blast of stale cigarette smoke from his compartment where they played cards. The blast of fresh air on the outdoor platform at the rear of the train. The intoxicatingly clear air and dark night and the promise of everything possible. The two of them, alone, now. The two of them, together, always. The possibility of that. How close he was. How handsome and near and possible and alive and bright and clear he was as he looked into her eyes and said . . . whatever it was he said.

And yet.

That was the thing. *And yet:* the thought that came to Carson one day, as she paced her room, running through the events on the train for the umpteenth time since her return home. It was a thought, and she couldn't just dismiss it. She'd had it; too late now. She could no sooner dismiss this thought—no sooner not pursue it—than she could the conversation with her uncle back in his office in Sintra. Once the possibility was there, there was no denying it, no pretending it wasn't what it was: a possibility. Simple as that.

Simple, simple, simple. Carson got up, balled her fist, pulled the hem of her bathrobe, and swung it so that it wrapped around her calves. *Nothing is simple*, she reminded herself.

So what was it? What was the thought? What was wrong with this picture?

The picture was this: the two of them, on the rear platform of a train as it raced through an anonymous night. Wind. Wine. Linen, brass, smoke, whist. The wind. Breaths coming shorter. So close. So *cold*. So suddenly cold. His coat, around her shoulders. The weight of it, of him, on her. So cold.

Cold, to her. Not to him. He's known cold. He's known poor. He's gotten past it. And now he's going to—how did he put it—"make a difference in the world."

"And are you making a difference?" Carson asked.

"I like to think I will," he answered, after giving the matter some thought, as if figuring out just how to phrase it.

No modesty now. For the first time all evening, a straightforward statement of intentions.

Or a statement of intentions, anyway. Just maybe not so straightforward.

And this was the thought that Carson grabbed hold of, as if she had indeed caught it in her little balled fist and couldn't let go. Yes, of course, modest little Alec Breve would like to use his knowledge of physics to make a difference in the world—and eager little Carson Weatherell would assume, as anyone in her position might, that the difference he wanted to make was the one *she* would want to make, if she were young and brilliant and a physicist at Cambridge in the runup to a war.

So, let her assume. Phrase it just so, so she'll think what she wants. State what you mean, and, for the first time all evening, don't be modest about it, because it's too great a source of pride, it's too central to your identity—to who you are in your heart of hearts. State what you mean so that you're true to yourself, but leave the meaning just open enough to others that they'll think what they want.

Sometimes Carson could punch that window with its stupid view of the stupid lawn. In the evening, the leaded glass gave back her reflection, and she didn't want to see that. So she shut off the lights. But she didn't stop pacing.

Because that was only the beginning, that ambiguous statement of Alec's on the train. There were more. Once Carson noticed one, others followed, like hidden pictures in one of those children's drawings. Once your eyes adjusted to what you were supposed to be seeing, the snakes came tumbling out of the trees.

When they confided in each other the intimacies of their life stories, and it was her turn to ask him what Cambridge was like, and he deflected her questions as expertly as he had those of her uncle that first night at dinner on board the train, she thought it was because he couldn't be bothered. She thought he, like she, didn't want to talk about the part of his background that interested him least. She, in her falling-in-love narcissism, thought he was just like her. And he allowed her—relied on her—to think that, instead of thinking the truth: he didn't want to talk about the part of his background that interested him most.

Or: the one time the four Cambridge scholars and Carson had sat around a bar in Lisbon drinking *caipiroscas* and discussing the political situation in the world, what did Alec have to offer? Carson thought hard about that afternoon, grateful she'd limited herself to one drink that day so she knew she could trust her memory now and come up with the exact answer to what Alec had added to that discussion weeks earlier: nothing. Everyone else weighed in. There was talk of the Fascists in Britain and Italy, talk of King Kong, talk of a German monster taking over the world, and all along Alec just sat there in silence, not simply impatient with any human interaction that didn't somehow allow him to draw closer to his lover, as Carson had interpeted his silence at the time, but unwilling to participate on any terms but his own. The monster waiting to take over the world? It was right there at their table, sipping, listening, waiting.

In the darkness of her room, following the path of moonlight along her carpet, Carson crossed to the window seat and slowly, slowly lowered herself to the cushion, and anyone who for any reason might have happened to be looking up at the grandest house in Marlowe, Connecticut, in the last days of August, 1936, would have seen a very frightened young woman—no: a very frightened girl—staring back.

CHAPTER SEVEN

The first letter arrived four days after she arrived home: a thin, sky-blue airmail missive covered with Alec's spidery, elegant handwriting.

"Darling girl," he wrote:

I've begun writing this the very second I've lost sight of you on the docks at Southampton so that it might reach you as soon as possible after your arrival in that faraway kingdom of Connecticut. Are you sitting in your room right now, that place you've described to me so well, with its peach-colored walls and white canopy bed? I can picture you there, truly, as well as your mum and dad. Is there any chance in hell that they might actually grow to like me, d'you think? Or will they simply see me as a poor-boy interloper who has corrupted their little girl and who hopes to take her from the bosom of the family? (The latter, I must admit, is also true. I *have* corrupted you, though not nearly as much as you've corrupted ME, with your creamy skin and heavenly touch— NOW STOP THIS, ALEC, IMMEDIATELY! MUST NOT DRIVE SELF MAD WITH LONGING—and I hope to continue doing so as long as we two may live.)

Oh, Carson, love, I miss you terribly. The damned unswimmable ocean separates us now, but please start thinking about when I might take a leave of absence from Cambridge and come stateside to be near you for a while.

I love you,
Alec

It was tempting to imagine, even if only for a moment, that the conversation with her uncle had never taken place, that the final three days in Portugal had passed in uninterrupted bliss, that Carson had returned to Connecticut breathlessly anticipating the arrival of precisely this kind of letter from her lover. But no: Carson reminded herself that she'd indulged enough fantasizing lately about what she'd hoped to have with Alec. Now, ignoring the slight shaking of her hand, she folded the letter back into its envelope and slipped it beneath the cushion of her window seat, where she used to hide her diary, and where she was certain Alec's letter would remain undiscovered.

Another letter arrived the following day, then another the day after that, and a fourth the day after that, all declaring his undying devotion. The day after *that*, Philippa Weatherell personally brought the mail upstairs to her daughter. There were two airmail envelopes, both of which she lightly tossed onto Carson's bed.

"These came for you," Philippa said in a casual voice that was, in actuality, anything but casual. "I gather they're from that boy your aunt Jane told us about."

That boy. Alec was hardly a boy, but Carson held her tongue. It was to be expected that Jane would tell her sister about the romantic interest in Carson's life, but she had to wonder exactly what Jane had said about the relationship. Carson couldn't be sure, but she felt that her aunt would have been protective of her niece's privacy. Which meant that, even if Jane suspected that Carson and Alec had become lovers, she wouldn't tell Carson's mother. That, if nothing else, came as a relief.

"Carson, darling," her mother continued now. "Your father and I have been talking. We can't help noticing how, shall we say, distracted you've been since you've returned from abroad."

"I'm fine, Mother," Carson tried.

"Sleeping late. Going to bed early. Spending most of the day in your bathrobe. And I—we; your father and I—we just want to say that however nice this boy might be, there *are* other boys out there."

"Like Harris Black," Carson said tonelessly.

"Well, yes, as a matter of fact," said Philippa. "Now, it's perfectly normal for someone your age to think that this boyfriend of yours is the only one for you, your one true love, but Carson, darling, I can tell you from experience that love doesn't work like that."

Carson groaned inwardly. "You don't understand," she said.

"Oh, I think I understand a good deal more than you give me credit for."

"Please," Carson said, turning to face her mother, "you really don't know what you're talking about." She could feel her cheeks starting to blaze as she spoke. "I'm breaking it off with him," she said.

Her mother stared at her for a moment, clearly taken aback. "Does he know that?" she asked gently. "I mean, he keeps writing to you, dear."

Carson shook her head. "No," she said. "He doesn't know that yet. I can't bring myself to write back. And if he calls, please don't put me through to him. Have whoever answers the phone say that I'm not home."

"Well, if you're not going to write to him, and you're not going to take his calls, when do you plan to tell him?" Philippa asked.

"I'm not sure," said Carson miserably. "I figure if I just don't answer his letters for a while, maybe he'll get the idea."

"Is that really fair to him?"

"He doesn't deserve my fairness," Carson said. Her mother looked puzzled, and Carson quickly went on. "I don't know what else to do, Mother. I've never been in this kind of situation, and I don't really know how to handle it."

Philippa walked over to Carson, and Carson allowed herself to be hugged by her mother.

"Do you want to talk about what happened?" Philippa asked, and Carson was taken aback by the tenderness in her mother's question. To Carson's surprise, there was no obvious judgment in Philippa's words. She seemed concerned with Carson's welfare, and little else—decorum be damned.

"Maybe," said Carson. "Maybe someday I'll tell you the whole story." She straightened up, and her mother released her. "But not now."

In fact, though, Carson wished just the opposite. She wished that she could tell Philippa everything, could simply pour out her heart to her mother the way she used to, but she knew that she couldn't, and not just because of the promise to her uncle. It was funny in a way, but Carson would have felt more comfortable confiding in her aunt. On the train ride back from Lisbon, Jane had offered her the opportunity to do just that, and Carson realized now, after her mother left her room and she was alone again, that if her aunt were here right this minute, she'd take her up on that offer—she'd tell Jane everything, regardless of Lawrie's orders. Carson wanted someone to talk to, but someone who had *lived,* who had taken chances and knew what it was like to risk everything for a love that would change your life forever.

In the absence of anyone to talk to, though, Carson found herself powerless to answer Alec—at least so far. And so instead, over the following week, she dispassionately read his letters, those long, earnest-seeming rambles that declared his love for her over and over, and she dodged his two telephone calls.

Had Alec ever really loved her? Had he merely used her to get to her uncle? Did he somehow love her, in his own way, during their most intimate moments of passion, or was she just some naive girl he'd met who had made his summer abroad pass more pleasantly? What did love even mean to someone like him? He must feel something; otherwise why would he keep up this assault from afar?

Maybe he really *did* love her; maybe he was one of those people who was able to split himself in two, so that one part of him could be a Fascist sympathizer and German supporter, while the other part could genuinely care for a young American woman. Carson had led a double life for three or four days, and it had depleted her. Alex was apparently able to do so indefinitely—and this was a more disturbing image than that of someone who was heartless and simply pretending to be in love. The split personality seemed more deadly, more corrupt. It reminded Carson of the way, when she was small, she'd found an earthworm that had been accidentally cut in half by a wheelbarrow in the garden, and how, even though it was now in two separate pieces, both halves lived on valiantly, squirming on the damp grass.

Wherefore, indeed.

One morning at nine A.M., Harris Black came calling. He'd telephoned several times since Carson had returned from her trip to Europe, but she'd always insisted she was busy, or unwell, or simply "fatigued." Finally it seemed to occur to Harris that he wasn't going to get anywhere by telephoning, and so he simply appeared at the door of the Weatherell house, dressed in tennis whites.

He was extraordinarily handsome, Carson was reminded as she looked him over, having been forced downstairs by her mother to say hello. ("Carson, if you don't go see this poor boy, I will be so mortified next time I see Miranda Black at the club, I don't know what I'll do!") There he stood in the marble foyer of the house, in his white shorts and white cotton V-neck sweater. His skin was tanned from a summer spent sailing and swimming and lounging on the Blacks' private spit of sand. He had a tennis racket slung over his shoulder casually, the way a soldier might carry a gun, Carson thought. War was certainly far from Harris's thoughts. She wondered if he worried at all about what was happening in Europe. Or, she thought, somewhat meanly, did he worry only about his backhand? And then Carson remembered that the last time she saw Harris, she'd been unfair to him then, too. It was on board the *Queen Mary*, when he and his parents had driven down from Connecticut to wish her bon voyage and he had lingered a moment in her stateroom to say he would see her when she returned, and Carson had corrected him: *You mean if I return.*

Who was that person? Carson wondered, not so much ashamed at the casual nature of her schoolgirl cruelty as at the innocence it implied. A comeback that she'd imagined to be the height of sophistication she now understood, from only a couple of months' distance, to be a transparent confession of insecurity.

In all fairness to Harris, Carson really had no idea how he viewed the world, and as she stood looking at him in the entryway of her house, something inside her took note of the fact that he was male, and very good-looking, a fact that she'd always known and had stored away. He smiled at her, a bright and warm smile that had the slightest tremor of uncertainty about it, and this made it touching. She realized that he wondered what she thought of him; clearly, he wanted to make a good impression. His own healthy looks matched hers, and his family's money was nearly as formidable as the Weatherell fortune. Carson imagined he wanted to spend time with her because it would be like coming home.

And that was the moment that Carson began to appreciate something she'd previously been able to acknowledge only on a rational, intellectual level: Alec Breve was not who he said he was. He was instead something she couldn't love. She should therefore be glad to be rid of him. It was that simple, and that complex—but it *was* that simple, too: Carson was, at long last, glad to be rid of Alec, if only a little.

Still, it was a start. She felt vaguely light-headed, as she usually did at such moments of clarity, but this time the feeling didn't disappear a moment later, swallowed inside the blackness of her longing for what might have been. Instead, the light-headedness lingered, like the relief that follows a high fever, so that when Harris asked her to play a set of tennis with him at the club that day, and then to have lunch with him, Carson answered, lightly, "Why don't you pick me up at noon?"

The cascade of letters from Alec piled up over the first two weeks of September on Carson's bureau, only now they remained unopened. She'd simply decided to stop reading them, and if she'd had any doubts about that decision, the last letter of his she'd read had eliminated them.

"Carson," he'd written (no "dear" this time):

Where in God's name have you gone? Either you're dead and no one can bear to tell me, or else you've dropped me from your life. I've telephoned your house several times and some servant has said you were out. Please call me and say you're all right.

Yours, as ever,
A.

She'd put the letter aside, still unwilling to answer. Somewhere in that same period Uncle Lawrence had called to ask about "the state of the relationship" between herself and

Alec. Tersely she repeated what she had told him on the dock in England, that she was done.

"You sound angry," said Lawrence across the crackling transatlantic connection.

"Angry? *Me?*" said Carson, and all of a sudden the feelings she hadn't been able to express to her uncle face-to-face began to come out. "That's a good one," she said. "You mean, just because the man I fell in love with is an informer and I've been trying to rat him out? Why, whatever gave you the idea that I'd be angry?"

"All right, Carson," her uncle said quietly. "I get the point. I'm very sorry that things worked out the way they did. I would never have gotten you involved in the first place if I wasn't positive it was important."

"Yet I was unable to give you any meaningful information," she said. "So what was the point, in the end?"

There was a long pause; all Carson heard was the static in the cables, and then finally her uncle said, "Look, there's another reason I'm calling. Jane has heard from Philippa that you haven't yet broken the news to Alec."

"So?"

"So," he went on, "don't you think it might be helpful if you did? By all means, yes, break it off with him, but I'm afraid too much of a delay will get him questioning things again. We don't want that."

"No, we don't," she answered drily.

"Then you'll do what's best?" he said.

"Yes," she answered, then added to herself: *What's best for me. Not for you. Not for Alec. For me this time.*

There was another long pause, and then her uncle offered

his apologies once again for getting her into this mess, and after Carson asked him to pass along her love to Jane, that was the end of the call. It wasn't until after she'd hung up the telephone in the downstairs library and retreated back up the stairs to her room that Carson realized she hadn't asked about Alec: whether they were planning to arrest him, or even, given the time lag between posting a letter in England and receiving it in the States, whether he was already in prison.

But why should she care? she reminded herself. The only advantage to knowing whether he was under arrest was that it might spare her the obligation of finally writing him the farewell letter she'd so long delayed. And write it she would, absolutely, one of these days. In the meantime, though, she was managing to distract herself through Harris Black.

If Alec Breve had stood for adventure, then Harris Black stood for its opposite. Under the circumstances, Carson didn't mind. In fact, she told herself, she preferred it. Harris would be heading off to Yale at the end of the September, but for now he and Carson had fallen into a pattern that Carson found pleasurable if unchallenging—or pleasurable precisely because it *was* unchallenging.

Nearly every morning Harris drove to her house and picked her up in his roadster, and they traveled the three miles to the Trelawny Country Club. There they played a set of tennis on the red clay courts, and then changed in the men's and women's dressing rooms and met in the grand Trelawny dining room for lunch. Under the glass atrium they sat and ate quivering little scoops of tomato aspic, and *blanquette* of chicken in a snowy white cream sauce, and for dessert they shared a tall peppermint ice cream parfait in a frosted silver cup.

Conversation did not exactly flow, but neither did it stall. Mostly, the two of them talked lightly about people they knew in common here in Marlowe, or of social events to come during the season. He'd be leaving for New Haven at the end of the month, but he'd be back often, he said, and he wanted her to be his date come December, for Yale's Winter Ball. Harris politely asked her questions about her time in Europe, and Carson noticed that if she went into any great detail while answering, he started to looked slightly bored. He would cover it as best he could, smiling and nodding encouragingly, but she could almost hear the thoughts circulating inside his brain: My, *she's pretty, but she does prattle on. I wonder whether I could get another helping of that ice cream?*

One morning they were joined by two friends of Harris's to play doubles and then have lunch. The couple, Christopher and Susan Hendrickson, were respectively seven and three years older than Harris and Carson; they had been married barely two months, and they lived one town away from Marlowe, in a Tudor house covered with vines that looked as though it ought to belong to a very old and stately couple, not to two vibrant people in their early twenties.

The Hendricksons were excellent tennis players, both of them smacking the ball with grace and precision. All four of the people on the court, in fact, had grown up playing tennis; it was a part of society life in Connecticut, though Carson had never particularly enjoyed the game. Sometimes she found herself trying to imagine Alec here among this crowd, and it was laughable. His racquet, if he even had one, would be old and slightly unstrung, and she was sure he would approach the game with his deadpan irreverence. Despite herself, she smiled at the image.

At lunch in the Trelawny Club dining room, the foursome sat under the glass and looked out over the golf course, where middle-aged men stood studiously over their five-iron clubs, patiently lining up their shots.

"So tell us," asked Christopher Hendrickson as the waiter filled everyone's water glasses, "how did you two meet?"

"Oh, we've known each other forever," said Harris. "Since grade school. Carson here was always the prettiest girl in school, and the most aloof."

"Objection," interrupted Carson.

"Overruled," said Harris. "But we never really got to know each other until recently, when she returned from Europe."

"Oh, did you go?" asked Susan. "I did, too. London, Paris, Rome, Madrid, Lisbon, the whole shebang."

"We stayed right near Lisbon," said Carson. "It was wonderful."

"Did you think so?" said Susan. "I preferred Paris. Lisbon was so . . . I don't know, I guess this sounds snobby, but it was unrefined. There were all these crumbling castles on hills around the edges of the city, and they looked like the failed soufflés our cook Betty used to make for us every Wednesday. Completely a shambles!"

"I liked them," Carson said quietly.

"And how about those performers," Susan Hendrickson went on. "I forget what they're called, but you know who I mean. Those strange men in cafés singing their love songs and hoping that some gullible Americans will put money in their hat."

"I was one of those gullible Americans," said Carson. "And they're called *fadistas*. They perform *fado*. It's an old tradition in Portugal."

Susan shivered melodramatically. "Well, I for one prefer the old traditions of Paris and London. The couture and the food and the shopping. Do you know, in Lisbon we saw quite a few women who had no teeth? How could they let themselves go around like that?"

Because they're poor, Carson wanted to say, but she said nothing. It was clear to her that this pretty and privileged young woman across the table had learned almost nothing from her trip to Europe.

"About half of the population thinks there's going to be a war," said Carson to no one in particular. "If Hitler keeps it up, then certainly there will be." This comment was met by a slightly puzzled silence. No one really had much to add. The two men nodded and muttered about "that damn Hitler," but neither seemed very engaged by the subject. Susan, in particular, seemed in over her head completely, and finally she simply changed the subject without even a hint of a segue.

"We saw Millicent Garner at Bendel's in Manhattan recently," she said in a bright voice. "We were both trying on the same dress to wear to the Diamond Ball."

"As you might gather, Susan likes the high life," Christopher put in with some apology and embarrassment in his voice. "Believe me, as her husband, the one who has to pay her Bendel's bills whenever she and her mother go on a shopping expedition into New York City, I'm well aware of her predilections."

Everyone laughed, except Carson, who simply took a long drink of ice water and wished the meal were over. She remained mostly quiet for the rest of lunch, and Harris looked over at her with concern. When the meal was through, and the men had fought over the bill in that way that men do (Harris won), and the women's chairs had been pulled back in a show of chivalry, the Hendricksons insisted that the foursome must get together again for tennis and lunch at the club "very, very soon." Then they pulled away in their baby blue MG roadster and went roaring down the road.

Harris and Carson sat for a few moments on the tufted moss stone wall that fronted the club.

"You weren't too happy at lunch," he finally said.

"I'm sorry."

"Don't be. I'm sorry about my friends," said Harris. "They're good people, really they are. Maybe not as exciting as you are."

"I wasn't aware that I was particularly 'exciting,' " Carson replied.

"Oh, yes," said Harris, and his face took on a sudden flush. "You can talk circles around me, Carson. I never knew that about you. I mean, as I told Christopher and Susan, you and I never really knew each other before. But ever since you came back from Europe, you seem somehow . . . different. Even more compelling."

She was surprised by his remark, and for a moment it made her less guarded. "I think I am different," she admitted.

"Seeing the world probably does that to you," he said. "I've traveled to Europe with my parents before, but to tell you the truth, I didn't really take all that much of it in. I was too young, I think, and my basic position was that if you've seen one headless or armless statue, you've seen them all."

Carson smiled. "It wasn't so much what I *saw* there, as what *happened* to me when I was there," she said, and she suddenly felt exposed. "I fell in love," she added simply, shocked that she'd revealed this to him, when just a moment before she'd had absolutely no wish to tell him or anyone this.

Harris looked down into his lap. He appeared vulnerable then, rather than shallow. "Oh," was all he said.

The old Carson, she realized, might have enjoyed his discomfort, might have seen it as part of a courtship ritual. Now, though, Carson felt the need to protect him, and without thinking, she said, "But it's over now."

He looked up at her in relief. *"Oh,"* he said again, and then, as if involuntarily, he smiled. "I mean, I'm sorry for you and everything, and if you ever want to talk about it—"

"No," Carson interrupted. "I don't think I will. But thank you, Harris."

"You don't have to thank me, Carson," he said.

They sat there awhile longer, listening to the leaves of the trees rustle and taking in the perfection of the day. It was nearly autumn now and the colors were starting their long, slow ceremonial fade along the autumn spectrum.

Carson understood, in that moment, that it was possible to get over a trauma in one's life and move on. The leaves changed every season because they were constantly in flux, never really one thing or another, and Carson supposed that this was a reasonable way to view her own life. You could fall in love with a man on a train traveling across Europe, only to find out that you had been misled. And instead of spending the rest of your life grieving about this painful episode, you simply let yourself move through it and into the next episode. You experienced the pain, you endured it; but in the end you moved past it, too. The leaf changed color slightly; one day it was yellow, and the next time you looked, it was red.

When Harris turned to her and touched her shoulder now, she knew what was going to happen, and she felt strangely passive, yet willing, too. This was so different from the kiss on the back of a train, with the night rushing by. She and Harris sat now in daylight, on a perfect fall afternoon, and he leaned forward and gently kissed her lips. She let him kiss her, didn't try to stop him, not because she felt overly aroused or curious, but because she didn't want to disappoint him, and because she was curious. His mouth tasted sweet and slightly cool from the peppermint parfait he'd eaten earlier, and she closed her eyes, trying as hard as she could to forget about that other mouth, that other kiss.

The next morning, Carson made the decision to write to Alec. The timing finally felt right—not for Alec, but for her. She had been able to prove to her own satisfaction that she really could move on. The next step was proving this to him so that he might, once and forever, leave her in peace.

"Dear Alec," she wrote in her careful, curlicued handwriting, though there was a slight tremor to her hand:

I know that I have been remiss in not writing you. Well, much more than remiss. I have been disgraceful, and for that I am sorry. Your letters and telephone calls have *not* fallen like trees in the forest. They've made a sound, all right, and it's me who's been trying to decide how to respond to that sound. Finally, I think I've decided.

Alec, what we had in Portugal was extraordinary. As you know, I'd never been in love with another man before, or even thought of any of the males I knew in Marlowe as "men." You were the first for me, in every way.

Since I've been back home in the States, I've had plenty of time to think about all that happened between us. I've come to the conclusion that I was swept up in what can only be thought of as a European "madness." Everything—the beautiful setting, the language, the strangeness—contributed to the excitement I felt when we were together. It wasn't just *you* who excited me. It was the atmosphere of Portugal as well. I'm so sorry to hurt you this way, but since I've been home in the very *unexciting* landscape of Marlowe, Connecticut, I can cast a cool eye over our relationship, and finally, objectively, see it for what it was: an adventure. Thank you for sharing that adventure with me. I will never forget it as long as I live.

But for now, I have to get back to a life that isn't built on some European fantasy. I've met someone else, Alec, someone here in town, who I've known for a long time. There, I've said it. Or written it, rather. Please know that I never meant to hurt you.

Yours,
Carson

When she was done, she sat and cried for a moment. It was a brief, strong cry, a needed release, and then she stood up and went to her bureau. Rooting quickly through the top drawer, she found what she was looking for: the thin bracelet with the tiny blue beads that Alec had given her in Portugal. She dropped it into the letter and quickly sealed it.

Carson placed the letter on the front hall table of her family's house, in the silver tray that contained outgoing mail. Later in the day, the housekeeper would take the mail to the post office in town while on her shopping rounds.

There. It was done. Carson felt relief, really, and when Harris picked her up that night to go out to a dinner dance at the Hendricksons', she was grateful to turn her thoughts away from Alec Breve, perhaps for good.

"For good," however, was a ridiculous assumption. The more you tried not to think about someone or something, the more you could not get it out of your mind. There had been a game she and her friends had once played at Miss Purslane's school. Don't think of the word *elephant*, one of the other girls had instructed everyone, and the girls had obediently closed their eyes and desperately attempted to let their thoughts land elsewhere. But elephants invariably appeared, trunks swaying. Right now Alec was that elephant. Perhaps he couldn't be banished, but at least over time, Carson hoped, his image would start to fade.

Harris helped. Sitting beside him in the front seat of his white roadster, driving down country lanes to the Hendricksons' party, Carson felt what it would be like to marry someone like him. You'd feel safe, she knew. Well, maybe not *entirely* safe, for some part of you would always be aware that Harris was really no stronger emotionally or intellectually than you were, and that he would need to be tended to and coddled over the years. Carson had never felt that way with

Alec. He had seemed strong and selfless and unpitying, all qualities that she'd admired, but which, in retrospect, had turned out to be illusory.

In the distance she could see the lights of the Hendricksons' party. Cars lined the road in the town of Barston Hills, and well-dressed couples in their twenties were laughing in the cool, dry night. "Hello, Harris!" someone called, and Harris said hello back, introducing Carson all around.

She could feel herself being sized up by other women, and looked over appraisingly by men. The glances, she could sense, were admiring. She fit in here. Some of these people knew her family, or at least knew of them. Others simply gathered, from her appearance and grooming, that she was "their kind."

And maybe I am, thought Carson. *Maybe I really am, after all*. She linked her arm through Harris's, and walked with him up the macadam drive and into the foyer of the Tudor house. Someone handed her a flute of champagne, and Harris led her inside.

They went on like that for two more weeks. There were other dinners at different young married couples' homes, and evenings spent at supper clubs. The days grew colder and the afternoon tennis games were abandoned. In one week Harris would be off to Yale, and Carson wondered what she would do with herself all day. One night at dinner she announced to her parents that she wanted to take a class of some sort, perhaps in a language, perhaps in court stenography, so that she would have some skills and could begin to look for a job.

"A job?" her father said when she brought this up. "Is that really essential?"

"I think so," Carson said quietly. "I'm getting bored, Daddy, just sitting around the house. And Harris is leaving any day now."

"There are plenty of things you can fill your day with," said her father. "Just ask your mother here." He turned expectantly to Philippa, but she seemed put on the spot.

"Oh yes," she said, "the days are very full, what with the club, and the charity season coming up, and all the work that needs to be done on the third floor of the house . . ." Her voice drifted off here, as though she realized that such activities would never be enough to sustain her daughter for a prolonged period of time.

"Well," Carson's father said, "if you're really interested in some sort of training, we'll have to think about it, all right?"

"All right, thank you, Daddy," Carson said. It was good enough for now. It would have to be. The problem with going off to Europe and having a love affair and then covertly working for British intelligence was that after you returned, the dimensions of your regular life might not seem adequate any longer. Being with Harris, to her surprise, was soothing. Soon, of course, he'd be at college; she pictured him in his dormitory room in Silliman at Yale, tossing a football idly in the air while he tried to focus on his studies. Harris promised to write to her once a week. The promise couldn't help but remind Carson of Alec's previous influx of letters, which had finally ceased.

Her letter to him must have done the trick. Alec must be over her, she thought, and if there was a sting of disappointment in this reasonable conclusion, Carson didn't want to dwell on it. Already she had begun to consign that whole part of her life to a distant closet in her mind, as if it were last season's fashions.

One night, she was lying in her bed after Harris had dropped her off at home; they'd just been to dinner at the Seaboard Grill, a dim but glossy restaurant with a fireplace roaring in the back and lobsters splayed on platters. Drinks had been liberally poured, and Harris entertained her with stories of the fraternity he planned to join at Yale, which his father and grandfather had belonged to before him.

After dinner, sitting in the front seat of his car, he'd reached out and kissed her more assertively than he'd ever done before, and then he moved closer so his body was against hers, and she could feel how substantial and lithe he was.

"Can we go somewhere?" he whispered. "Somewhere private?"

"Not yet," she whispered back.

"I want you so much," he said.

"I know," she said softly, almost sympathetically. "Still, let's wait."

"All right," he said. "Of course." He pulled away, steadying himself, straightening his tie, coming to his senses. "I got a little carried away," he admitted. "Being with you does that to me. I've never been this way. There's been no one before you, Carson."

She didn't answer him, though not to be cruel. To be kind, in fact, to spare Harris from hearing that, yes, there had been someone before him—that fellow she'd mentioned once, the one she'd fallen in love with over the summer. That, yes, his girlfriend hadn't "waited."

But what, exactly, was she waiting for now? Not for marriage, certainly, for she hadn't felt the need to wait for that with Alec. And not for "love" either, for Carson knew that what she felt for Harris Black right now was probably the extent of what she could ever feel for him. A strong, uncomplicated *like,* mixed with real physical attraction. Many marriages, such as her parents', were built on far less. But in Carson's mind, she wanted to wait to make love to Harris because what she felt for him really wasn't enough to justify such intimacy. When would it be enough? Perhaps never. For now, all she could say was "Let's wait," and Harris assumed she was being honorable, and moral, and this probably made him want to make love to her even more.

That night, after he'd said a lingering good night to her on the Weatherells' front porch, Carson went upstairs slowly and quietly, not wanting to disturb her parents. In her own bedroom, she lay down on the bed, her pale pink skirt flowering all around her, and for the longest time she just lay there, unwilling to get up yet. The scene with Harris had left her uneasy—not because of what he'd wanted from her, but because it reminded her that the reprieve Harris Black had offered her from her own worries and concerns was drawing to an end. In three days he would be motoring off to Yale. Three days: the same amount of time that with Alec she had hoped would last forever, until she had prayed for it to pass in the blink of an eye. Now the three days remaining before Harris left her seemed like . . . three days, actually. Carson's thoughts drifted to that job she'd mentioned to her parents. She thought about Harris's visits home from Yale in the fall. She thought about helping her mother with charity work and—

what was it her mother had said? Something that needed to be done on the third floor of the house?

Suddenly Carson heard a spray of pebbles at her window. *It must be Harris,* she thought. *Perhaps he's decided he can't wait, after all.* Carson went to the window and wearily pushed both halves open. There, down below, standing on the lawn and looking up at her in the thin light, stood a figure. She was about to call down to him, when her eyes began to adjust and she saw that it wasn't Harris Black down there.

It was Alec Breve.

CHAPTER EIGHT

All she could think about, looking down at him in astonishment from her second-story window, was the balcony scene in *Romeo and Juliet*. In Shakespeare's play, Romeo had come to Juliet's house to profess his love to her and be near her. But here, on this chilly night in 1936 in Connecticut, Alec had traveled all the way across the Atlantic Ocean to . . . to do what? Carson had no idea. To wreak revenge? Had he somehow discovered that during their final days together she was reporting back to her uncle his every movement, almost? She was so shocked by his presence that she could hardly speak. For a moment she just stayed where she was, framed by her window, still peering out at Alec, who looked so small down below.

"Carson," he said in a voice so soft she could barely hear it. "I have to talk to you."

She didn't know whether to slam the window and call for help or to play it cool. Then it occurred to her that if she slammed the window and called for help, she might never learn why Alec had come all this way.

"What are you doing here?" she hissed.

"You know what I'm doing here," he hissed back. "All

those letter and calls. I had to find out for myself what was going on."

That was why? Not because he'd been exposed as a Nazi sympathizer, but because he'd been jilted?

"I wrote you two weeks ago," she said, recovering. "Didn't you get it?"

"Yes, I did. But I didn't believe it."

"Well, believe it."

"I'm beginning to, after what I've seen tonight."

"What?" she said, thrown again. "What have you seen?"

"Your new . . . boyfriend. Out front earlier. Saying good night."

Carson felt herself flush. "Were you *spying* on me?" She opened her mouth to say more, then realized the irony of being indignant at Alec spying on *her*. "Oh, this is absurd," she said. "All right. Wait a little while. Go for a walk or something. My parents usually go to bed in about half an hour. I'll meet you by the greenhouse over there," and she pointed past a bank of trees.

He hesitated, then nodded and disappeared into the darkness. She sat in her room anxiously, barely moving, not knowing what she was doing or what was about to happen. She tried to organize her thoughts, to come up with a plan of some sort. But she had no idea what to expect from Alec, and so she had no way to prepare herself, and instead she simply sat there, on the edge of the bed, her hands folded in her lap, as if by being the very picture of calm, she might actually become calm.

Half an hour later, like clockwork, her parents' bedroom light snapped off. Downstairs, the housekeeper was sponging down the kitchen counters and yawning. In a moment, Carson heard her pad off up the back stairs to the servants' quarters. Slowly, quietly, wearing a cloth coat over her pink dress, Carson descended the front stairs. She could hear the gentle ticking of the grandfather clock in the living room, as well as the slight settling of the wood of the house that she'd heard throughout her life when she was trying to sleep at night. Without a sound, Carson walked through the house, headed to the back door, and opened it. There, across the lawn, sitting on the stone bench in front of the small greenhouse her father had installed just last summer, Alec waited for her. As she came closer, she could see him much more clearly than from above. He wore a thick black cable-knit sweater and carried a rucksack slung over his arm, like some merchant seaman who'd been traveling for months.

He stood at her approach. She pointedly stopped a good ten yards from him.

"All right," she said. "I'm here. What do you want?"

"I want to know why you've done this," he said. "I just don't understand it."

"I told you," Carson said, unable to meet his eyes. "I had time to think it all through. It was just a summer romance."

"It was *not*," said Alec angrily. "I refuse to believe that you feel this way. I've racked my brain again and again, trying to come up with what I've done, what could possibly have turned you away from me like this. I tell myself: It's that other man, she's in love with him, but then I remember that it was in *Portugal* that you started acting strange. And then things got better again near the end, but something had shifted. The balance was off, or something, and it never quite recovered for the rest of our stay. I told my friends about it, and they thought I was daft. Michael said you were the best person of the female persuasion to come along in my life since he'd known me, and Freddy said you were perfect, for a Yank, and Tom told me I was boring them to death with my paranoid fantasies that you didn't love me anymore even though you said you did."

Carson didn't say anything. She just stood trembling in the watery light from the greenhouse, listening to what he had to say.

"I've never felt this way about a woman before," he went on. "And you *are* a woman, not a little girl, even though when you came abroad you wanted to cling to childhood as long as you could. So maybe that's what you're doing again, is that it? Clinging to childhood one more time, because it's been taken away from you. Because I stole your innocence, is that how you see it? Because I made love to you and *you liked it.*"

His words seared right through her. She knew she shouldn't say a word, but should simply absorb everything he was accusing her of, letting him think he was right. But she felt wrongfully accused. After all, it was Alec, wasn't it, who had ruined everything?

He began to walk toward her.

"Don't," she said. "I mean it, Alec. Stop. Stop right there or I'll call for help, I swear I will, Alec."

He stopped. They were still several paces apart.

"Call for help?" he said. "What has gotten into you? It's only me. Alec."

"Whoever that is," she said before she could stop herself.

"What? What's that supposed to mean?"

"*You* know," said Carson, looking down at the ground, slightly surprised that she'd done this, the one thing she'd promised her uncle she would not do, but slightly relieved, too.

Alec started to take a step toward her, then stopped himself. "No, I *don't* know," he said, and his face was twisted up in a way that she'd never seen before. He was almost spitting the words now, his voice a combination of anger and pain. Carson couldn't be sure, but he seemed to be on the verge of tears. "I can't stand it. I can't take this anymore, Carson. Tell me. *Tell* me."

Carson closed her eyes, took a deep breath, opened her eyes. "*That you're a Fascist and a member of the Watchers and are giving information to Germany,*" she said in a rush.

There. She'd done it. In the long silence that followed, she studied Alec's reaction closely.

He just looked at her. He seemed to be studying her in return, regarding her strangely, slowly. Now he knew that she knew his secret. What would he do about it? she wondered. Oddly, she didn't feel afraid at all. Whatever happened, happened. She was far past really caring now. Blurting out the truth to Alec hadn't been something she'd planned, but whatever Alec had to say to her now would apparently be equally unscripted and unrehearsed. From the heart, if only he'd had one.

All right. So now you know, she thought he might say, his voice low and challenging, his figure advancing on her in the dark. Or maybe, *How did you find out?* in the matter-of-fact manner of the criminally insane.

But instead he just looked at her and said, "That is the most absurd thing I've ever heard in my life."

She looked back at him, neither of them even blinking. He didn't look challenging; he didn't look menacing. He looked almost . . . puzzled.

"I don't believe you," she said.

"It's true," said Alec. "I hate those Fascists, those Mosleyites, with their black shirts, marching around in imitation of Hitler. And I'm not crazy about the Germans either. For God's sake, Carson, they killed my father."

"They did? You never told me that," she said, suddenly thrown once again.

"I don't like to talk about it much," he said. "Look, my father *was* a drunk. But he was also a soldier. He enlisted during the last war. He fought hard and then he died for England. A German soldier stabbed him with a bayonet and he bled to death. My father might have been drunk at the time; I hope he was, actually, so that he didn't feel the pain so badly." Alec took a breath. "I grew up with that," he said. "My whole life has been shadowed by it. And you have the gall to say that I'm a spy for the Germans. I will give my life to defeat the Germans if England goes to war—no, *when* England goes to war. Because I think I've come to agree with your uncle, that war is precisely where we're headed."

Alec's face, when he spoke, was hard and furious.

"I don't understand," Carson tried. "Either you're the best liar in the world or my uncle is wrong."

"Your uncle?" said Alec. "He's the one who told you this lie?"

It was too late to back down now, Carson knew. She'd done everything she swore to Lawrence she wouldn't, and yet there had been no choice. Who'd have thought that Alec would have traveled across the Atlantic to confront her face-to-face?

"He said there was proof," said Carson. "Definite proof."

"What proof?"

"He wouldn't say. Couldn't say. He said it was classified."

"And that's when your whole attitude toward me started to change, back in Portugal?"

Carson lowered her eyes and nodded her head. Then she looked him in the eye again. "My uncle said this evidence, whatever it is, definitely links you to the Watchers."

"You can't be serious," Alec said, running his hand through his hair and half turning in a circle. "This can't be happening. Those people are fanatics. And their hatred of Jews?" He turned back to Carson and held out a hand, pleadingly. "I've known Jews my entire life. The past couple of years, as this whole Fascist nonsense has spread through England, I've even gotten into a couple of fistfights over anti-Semitic remarks. And did you know that Mrs. Bertram—the woman who put me through Cambridge—is Jewish? Look at me, Carson. Do you really think that I'm capable of the things you've accused me of?"

She looked him full in the face. There, in the spill of light, she took in the sheer despair of his features, the magnitude of it, unadorned and removed from pretense. He was either telling the truth or he was a liar beyond human comprehension—or her comprehension, anyway.

"Why should I trust you?" she finally said.

"I can't answer that," he said softly. "Only *you* can answer that."

Trust. That word again. Carson had tried to learn to trust herself this summer, but after that fateful conversation with her uncle about Alec, she'd decided that she'd made a terrible error in judgment. So she had trusted her uncle, instead. But what if *that* had been a terrible error in judgment? What if she had been right about Alec all along, right from the start, right from that first night on the train to Lisbon? What if the Ministry of Defence had made some mistake?

Carson considered her options. Her uncle had told her one thing, and now Alec was telling her another. Only one story could be true. She could trust her uncle, or she could trust Alec.

Or, she slowly realized, she could just trust herself. Not trust or distrust Lawrence. Not trust or distrust Alec. Just trust herself, moment by moment, step-by-step, however long it might take, however difficult it might be, until she'd reached the truth.

Carson took that first step now. Tentatively she made a move forward, toward Alec, and then he, freed from his frozen position, took a step, and then the two of them rushed together. Carson threw her arms around his neck and Alec wrapped his hands around her waist. Touching him again was such a relief; she could feel it in her body, a kind of catharsis, as though she'd been holding her breath all this time. She kissed him then, hard, hungily, and it was like being released from a spell, like waking herself up from a hundred-year sleep. Carson wasn't naive. She knew it was possible that she was making another terrible error in judgment.

But she didn't think so.

She was being given a second chance, that's what she believed. It wasn't often in life that you got one of those, yet here it was, waiting for her like an unclaimed gift.

Suddenly Alec pulled back. "Oh, I almost forgot," he said, breaking their embrace. He fumbled in his pocket for a moment, then produced an object, which he held out to her.

It was her bracelet. The one he'd given her in Lisbon, and which she'd sent back to him through the mail. Here it was again, with its delicate chain and tiny blue beads. He slipped the bracelet onto her wrist.

"Oh, Alec," she whispered, her eyes shining. She reached up to touch his face, and the bracelet slid slightly down her arm. "I can't believe this is happening. I can't believe you're really here."

"I know," he said. "I can't either," he added, and he laughed. "I suppose it *was* a bit extreme, coming over here. But it was the only chance I had. Nobody believed me. None of my friends, anyway. Nobody but Mrs. Bertram." Alec explained how he'd told Mrs. Bertram that the nice American girl he'd been promising to bring back with him to Bloomsbury had mysteriously discarded him, and how he'd told her the only way he could believe it was true was to hear it from Carson herself, and how Mrs. Bertram had promptly offered to pay Alec's way to the States. "I think I caught the very next ship out of Southampton, literally," Alec said now, and he laughed again. But then his expression darkened. He pulled away from Carson slightly and peered down at her. "You said your uncle is convinced I'm passing information to the Germans," he went on.

"Yes."

Alec blew out a breath. "This is damn serious business, Carson. I'm in way over my head here. Perhaps if I spoke to him—"

Carson cut him off. "That won't do any good. If he won't listen to me, he's certainly not going to listen to you. In fact," she went on, hesitantly, "if he knew I told you what he'd told me, I think he'd have you locked up."

"Locked up," Alec echoed dully. "So if I can't speak to him, what *can* I do?"

"You mean, what can *we* do?"

Alec smiled crookedly, pulling her close for another kiss. Then he rested his cheek against hers.

"So," he whispered, "what are you thinking?"

"I'm thinking," she answered, "that it's time Mrs. Bertram and I finally got to meet."

Before he could respond, she took Alec by the hand and led him to the bench by the greenhouse. There they sat shoulder to shoulder in the cool night air as she began to describe what they should do now.

This would be Carson's plan. Just as her uncle had orchestrated the final three days in Portugal and, in a way, the days and months that followed, so Carson now conceived the way the next week would work. As for how her plan might affect the days and months that followed—might alter the very lives that depended on its success—she couldn't say. "But," she said, "there's only one way to find out."

If she was right, she told Alec, British intelligence knew that Alec was visiting her right now. There was no chance that they had let a suspected traitor leave England without

monitoring his movements closely, and when word reached
Lawrence that after Alec Breve had reached New York he'd
headed straight for Connecticut, there wouldn't be any question of his destination. And who knew? she added. Lawrence
might have already sent word that the local authorities should
pick up the two of them at once, and police cruisers might at
that moment be charging across the back roads of Connecticut toward the Weatherell house. Or maybe the authorities
were waiting for daylight to make their move. The point was,
Carson said, she and Alec might never get the chance to put
their plan into action, and they must prepare themselves for
that possibility. But then again, she said, maybe they would,
and they'd better prepare for that possibility, too.

And that plan was this: The two of them would head
down to New York at once, check the shipping news in the
morning papers, and book passage on the first available liner
sailing for Southampton. Mrs. Bertram had provided Alec
with sufficient funds for his return passage, of course, and
when Carson said she could stop by the bank and withdraw
some money for her own ticket, Alec said that wouldn't be
necessary—that Mrs. Bertram had provided him with enough
money to purchase a ticket for Carson, too, "just in case
things worked out." Perfect, Carson said when she'd heard
this; the less documentation they left behind, the better their
chances for reaching their ultimate destination. Which was,
she announced to Alec, not Cambridge, where Alec would be
vulnerable to all sorts of insinuations or accusations about access to sensitive information, but the neutral—and nurturing—
London home of Mrs. Bertram.

"Brilliant," Alec said. "And then what?"

"And then," Carson answered, sitting straighter, somewhat surprised at this sudden flight of improvisation on her part, "I guess I'll have to think of something else."

The dome of the British Museum glowed in the sunlight just as Alec had always promised it would, when the day eventually came that he would escort Carson along the quiet and refined streets of Bloomsbury to the white-pillared house of Mrs. Bertram. England itself seemed to be gleaming on this day, and Carson thought wistfully how magical the occasion would have seemed if this visit were taking place under happier circumstances, the kind that she and Alec had always imagined. But it wasn't, and in the new spirit of trusting herself moment by moment, step-by-step, Carson instead resolved to make the most of the visit, no matter what.

They hadn't cabled or telephoned Mrs. Bertram in advance. Carson worried that the authorities would intercept the message, learn where they were heading, and perhaps pay Mrs. Bertram a visit first—a frightening prospect, considering that the news that the British government suspected Alec of passing information to a foreign government was sure to come as a considerable shock. Better that she hear it from Alec himself than from some plodding Sherlock operating according to his own agenda.

So it was with even more trepidation than the situation might otherwise warrant that Carson waited while Alec first leaned on the doorbell. He cleared his throat. He tightened his grip on her arm, giving her elbow a reassuring squeeze. Carson glanced over her shoulder in both directions, as if she might be able to discern which of the many pedestrians strolling toward or away from the museum, or which of the several automobiles trolling the narrow street or parked at a discreet distance, might be the one keeping tabs on the two of them. An involuntary shudder ran up her spine, ending at the back of her neck.

"Cold?" Alec said.

"Nervous," Carson answered.

She'd had a week to prepare herself for this moment, and it still seemed unreal. It was frustrating, to say the least, to have to wait six days to reach the other side of the ocean. Daredevil pilots in airplanes could manage the crossing in just over half a day now, and paying customers aboard zeppelins could actually make the trip in relative comfort, as long as they were willing to begin their voyage in New Jersey and terminate it in Germany, neither of which would have been helpful to Carson and Alec. And so for the third time in as many months Carson had found herself staring out at the Atlantic and counting the days until she reached the far shore.

She had made one complete rotation since the summer began, going from loving Alec to hating him to loving him again, or at least leaving herself open to that possibility. She still had her doubts. How could she not? Her own uncle had convinced her once of Alec's duplicity, and he might yet convince her again.

What if he's still lying? she wondered one morning, lying in bed in their stateroom, watching Alec button a shirt. *What if he's manipulating me?* Well, what if? If he was lying to her, she would find out soon enough, and she would have to absorb that blow once again. But in the meantime, she could only try to learn to trust herself, and for now, in this moment, she trusted herself to be here with him.

From time to time during that week at sea she'd thought of Harris Black, of course. On the evening of the day she'd left, Harris was supposed to be taking her out to dinner and to see the new Carole Lombard comedy at the Bijou, something about her posing as a princess on a transatlantic trip. Somehow, now, Carson didn't think that plot sounded so funny. Harris was a good man; he didn't deserve to be treated this way, and she wondered if he would ever forgive her. By now, she supposed, he would be leaving for college, and Carson hoped for his sake that he would meet a girl at a dance, someone from Radcliffe or Smith or Wellesley who could love him in a way that she could not.

And Carson thought about her parents. She imagined her mother throwing herself into whatever work it was she wanted to do on the third floor, utterly incapable of understanding a daughter who would have the nerve in every sense of the word to flee in the middle of the night. That last night in Marlowe, Carson had shakily come back inside the dark, sleeping house long enough to pack one bag and leave a note. The words, written on a piece of scrap paper she'd found in the drawer of the front-hall telephone table, didn't come easily to her, for she knew the upsetting effect they would inevitably have in only a few hours' time:

Dear Mother and Daddy,
I have gone away for a while, with someone I need to be with; I'm really not sure how long I will be. Please please PLEASE don't worry about me. I'm not in any trouble, but

there is something I simply need to do. I know this is difficult for you, but I promise that I will be in touch with you as
soon as I can. I only hope that you trust me to make the decisions that are right for me. Remember, I'm not a child anymore. Please tell Harris that I'm very, very sorry, and that I
didn't mean to hurt him.

> I love you both,
> Carson

Then she'd added a two-word P.S.: "Trust me." And she'd
underlined the word *trust* three times.

But mostly during that week at sea she'd thought about
Alec. As she embraced Alec on the lawn that night in Marlowe, her old feelings for him had flooded back to her at once;
they were important feelings, essential feelings, but they were
also basic feelings, arising from a fundamental human need.
Only now, on the ship, as she and Alec took advantage of the
leisurely pace and the middle-of-nowhere seclusion to catch
up with each other in the same all-day-together way they had
at the Pensão Moderna, could a more complex set of feelings
emerge, those of comfort and security and, more than anything, belonging.

Those final three days in Portugal, and then even on the
return voyage from Europe, Carson had tried to protect herself by steeling herself against her own emotions, by isolating
them, as if her feelings for Alec somehow existed outside herself. Then, when she was safely alone in her bedroom back in
Marlowe, she had allowed herself to experience those emotions fully, surrendering to them, letting her grief and anger
engulf her, until she was afraid she might never resurface. But

now, back in Alec's arms, she understood that although she'd experienced those feelings fully, she hadn't experienced them *completely*. She needed someone to hear them, but not just anyone: not her worried but judgmental mother; not the sympathetic but uncomprehending Harris Black; not even her worthy aunt Jane, Carson saw now; and surely not her own untrustworthy self, going over and over recent events as she paced back and forth in her bedroom. It was Alec she needed. Only Alec. Her thoughts and fears and hopes and grief and even anger at him were only approximations of what she felt, until he'd heard them. It was like when they made love in the Pensão Moderna, or now on board the ship; both of them kept their eyes open so they wouldn't miss a moment, so they would see each other's changing expressions. Did other lovers do that? She had no way of knowing. All she knew was that it was what she did with Alec—and that she wasn't complete until she saw herself in Alec's eyes.

And so one afternoon on board the ship, the ocean gently rocking them in its lullaby rhythm, the sunlight through the porthole casting rippling patterns across their naked bodies, Carson stared up into Alec's eyes, saw them burning back into hers, and she knew: *I believe you.*

The massive door budged once with the effort of someone on the other side trying to tug it open. Carson and Alec exchanged glances, wondering if one of them should offer to help Mrs. Bertram open her own front door. It budged again, and then it finally freed itself from the doorframe, swinging wide.

Perhaps because Alec had always described Mrs. Bertram

as a vital person, purposeful and opinionated, Carson had been expecting a large woman, a battleship. To Carson's surprise, however, Mrs. Bertram was a tiny woman, "birdlike," as Carson thought a novelist might write. She wore a pale blue angora sweater draped around her shoulders and a pair of pince-nez perched on the bridge of her nose. Her hair was beautiful, Carson thought, a weave of silver and auburn, tied loosely in a bun but with sprays of tendrils framing a lovely, kind face that just now, taking in the unlikely, unexpected sight awaiting her on her doorstep, expanded into a radiant smile.

"Oh, my sweet boy," she said softly, and she came forward to embrace Alec and kiss him European style, on both cheeks. "I am so very glad to see you." Then she turned her attention to Carson.

"This is Carson," said Alec. "Carson Weatherell."

"Of course," Mrs. Bertram said. "I would know her anywhere. She is just as you described her."

"Hello, Mrs. Bertram," Carson said, reaching out her hand. Mrs. Bertram clasped it and smiled. She continued to hold Carson's hand, appraising her, her head tilting as if regarding a painting in a museum. Carson waited, watching, knowing somehow that this moment *mattered*. Here was a woman who had been crucial in Alec's life, someone who had given him love and values and a Cambridge education. Carson wanted Mrs. Bertram to feel that here was someone who would be just as good for Alec as she herself had been. "I've heard so much about you," Carson offered.

"Oh, I'm sure I've heard much more about *you*," Mrs. Bertram replied. "I've known Alec a very long time, and believe me, I've never heard him say half this much about any other young woman. And I can see why. You dazzle the eyes, and no doubt the heart."

"I'm so sorry we didn't call ahead," Alec said, but Mrs. Bertram waved his apology away as if it were a minor irritant, a flying insect.

"You always have a room here," she said. "You know that, dear. One doesn't call home simply to say one is coming home, now does one? This is a pleasant surprise—so pleasant, in fact, it would appear I've forgotten my manners. Come in, come in."

The interior of the house was, if possible, even grander than Carson had imagined. Though it was located in the middle of a city, with other houses on either side, Mrs. Bertram's home was really a mansion. A marble staircase lined one wall of the foyer, while doorways along the hall offered views of various rooms, each glittering with antiques. The Persian rugs were soft underfoot, the walls were the color of cream, and everything smelled of rose water and lemon polish

Mrs. Bertram led them into the parlor, and before long all three of them were sitting together drinking tea, eating ginger biscuits, and talking intensely. Carson and Alec explained the entire story to Mrs. Bertram, who listened keenly, nodding and asking questions every once in a while. When they'd finished telling her everything, she put down her teacup and leaned her head back, eyes closed, hands clasped in her lap, as if in deep thought. Finally, she spoke.

"I know a gentleman," she said slowly, "who might be of some help to you. His name is Lord Aidan Roberts, and he was an old and very dear friend of my late husband, Harold. They were commanders together in the Royal Navy during the last war. He now works in Special Intelligence, and if anyone would have access to information such as this, it would be Lord Aidan. I feel certain that he will be able to find out exactly how Alec has been implicated, where the investigation stands at the present time, and what steps need be taken to go about clearing his name. Alec hasn't been charged with anything, of course, which makes it a more complex matter. And whether or not Lord Aidan is willing to reveal any of this information to me is another story." She paused for a moment, and then said, "I shall pay him a visit at his offices this very week. I need to get out a little more anyway; my physician says it will do my heart a world of good."

Carson had to hide a smile. She now understood that beneath the quaint and gentle elderly-woman exterior there waited a surprisingly observant and cunning woman. *Wherefore art thou Mrs. Bertram?* she thought, and Carson realized that such was her hostess's grace and authority, she felt warm and safe and welcome in this house, as if *she* were the one coming home, not Alec.

That night, Alec showed Carson to a guest bedroom on the third floor. The room was done up in royal blue and white, with a plush blue satin comforter and a picture window that looked out upon the spires of London. Alec's own room was down at the other end of the hall.

"I'll miss you all night," he whispered into her hair as they stood in the center of her room. "I wish we could be together."

"I know," she said, wishing equally that they could spend the night together, lying in the depths of her bed. But then they did what they had to do, regretfully separating for the night, giving each other last-minute kisses.

A short while later there was a light knock at Carson's door. She was standing and brushing her hair before the antique oval mirror above the bureau. She put down the heavy silver brush and went to answer it. Mrs. Bertram stood there in the late-night hallway, dressed in a nightgown and yellow silk robe.

"I'm sorry to disturb you," began Mrs. Bertram, "but I saw the light on beneath your door. And I saw the light on beneath Alec's door as well . . ." She let her words drift off purposefully here, though Carson didn't know what she was supposed to infer from them.

"Oh," she said. "Did you want me to shut off my light, is that it? Am I wasting electricity? Because I never meant—"

But Mrs. Bertram simply laughed. "Of course not," she said. "Look, it's absolutely none of my business, you understand, and feel free to tell me to keep out of it, but I suppose I just don't understand why you and Alec are not . . . well, together tonight. After all, were you not together on the ship?"

Carson gazed at the elderly woman. Mrs. Bertram wore a puckish expression, and Carson could not quite take in the message all at once, but as far as she could tell, the very proper and distinguished Mrs. Bertram was saying to Carson, *Go to him. Spend the night with him in my house. He is the man you love, and I know one or two things about love myself.*

"Thank you," said Carson softly, and Mrs Bertram simply nodded and retreated down the stairs, her slippers barely making a sound on the carpeted treads.

Within thirty seconds, Carson was knocking on Alec's door, and soon she was climbing into his bed beside him. "But what about Mrs.—" he said, and she put a finger to his lips, shushing him, telling him that it was all right, that Mrs. Bertram was a most accommodating hostess. He reached up to shut off the night-table lamp, and then they were together once again in darkness, and a warm bed, and each other's arms. Tomorrow, who knew where the story would lead? Who knew where it would eventually end? Tonight, though, it would end where bedtime stories always do: happily ever after.

CHAPTER NINE

This week," she'd said, referring to when she would call on Lord Aidan, as if time were not of the essence, but in fact the following morning Mrs. Bertram appeared in the living room in a blue wool suit, mentioned she would be heading over to Whitehall as casually as if she'd said she needed to stop at the local apothecary, and urged Alec and Carson to make themselves at home.

After she left, disappearing into the London rain with an umbrella and an unmistakable sense of purpose, Carson and Alec quickly agreed that they couldn't bear the thought of simply sitting around the house waiting for Mrs. Bertram to return with some news of his fate. And so they set out into the light London rain themselves, two people making their way in the world under one black umbrella, and together they walked the streets aimlessly until they came to the pub of an inn called The Rose and Stag. Inside, Alec blew into his cupped hands and ordered a breakfast of "bangers and mash" for the both of them.

"It looks as exotic as anything I ate in Portugal," Carson said when the plates arrived. She was using a knife to poke at the glistening, spicy sausages, as if they were some sort of specimen in biology class.

"British food isn't known for its exotic elements, or for its tastiness, to put it mildly," said Alec. "But this is what I grew up eating, and I have to say, I do have a soft spot for it."

Carson smiled and, as she'd learned to say, "tucked in" to the meal. "Tell me about the war," she said a moment later, changing the subject suddenly, getting down to the business of what she wanted to discuss.

"What war?"

"The next one," she said. "You think it's coming, you told me. You think there's no way to stop it from happening."

Alec nodded. "Yes, I do think it's coming," he said. "I think it's inevitable. I'll never be able to understand the aggressiveness and territoriality of Hitler. And the prejudice against Jews and immigrants—anyone who's different—well, that speaks for itself. Growing up poor in London, with a charwoman for a mum, I faced a good amount of prejudice myself. People thought that because we were poor, we were somehow *dirty*. When in actuality my mum was one of the cleanest people I knew, and she kept our tiny little flat as neat as a pin. The world is basically just one long food chain," Alec went on, "with people gobbling up whoever's just below them. Germany mobilizes its citizens to think it's not the economy or the policies of their government that's making their lives so economically bleak. Oh no, it's the *Jews*, and the tide of unwashed immigrants, of course; what else could it be?"

He ate a forkful of bangers, and washed them down with a swig of hot, sweet tea. "There are plenty of Britons who have no love for anyone other than their own elitist selves, of course," he added. "*Plenty*. The Watchers are among them.

But unlike some of their outspoken and aboveboard brothers, they operate in secret, working within the system, within elite corridors, keeping their identities hidden so that they can transmit ideas and defense plans more easily to Germany. They believe that though they're against it, war may be inevitable, and if it is, they want to be on the right side when victory comes."

Alec pushed away his plate suddenly. "I can't eat any more," he said. "I've no appetite after having this conversation. The idea that someone would say I was a member of those bloody Watchers—the idea that *my* name is on a list in some government office, that *I'm* being watched myself and considered a traitor to my country—is hateful to me."

She held his hand tightly across the table, and they sat in silence in the pub for a few moments. His anguish was her own now; that was what being in love did to you. This was something she'd never known before, for when they'd first fallen in love, all that they'd shared had felt bathed in a golden light. And then, when they'd parted, all that they'd shared had felt ruined, rotted, like old fruit, but those were feelings that Carson had endured alone. Now she'd arrived at a third alternative: she and Alec had left behind the golden glow of first falling in love, yes, but they had left it together. And now, together, they were entering reality: eating bangers and mash in a London pub and talking about injustice.

"I believe you, you know," she reminded him softly. "I really do."

"I can't imagine why you would," Alec said. "You've no proof I'm not who they say I am. You've only got my word against theirs."

"It doesn't matter." She shook her head slightly. "I can't explain it," and the fact was, she couldn't. It had something to do with intuition, with a certainty deep inside—with learning to trust yourself. That moment on the ship when she'd realized she truly believed Alec? She saw now that it was actually the moment when she finally knew what she'd in fact known all along, which was what she'd been talked out of by her uncle, despite her better judgment. And she saw now that what had changed in her literal moment of truth— that moment of recognizing and accepting what she'd known to be true all along—had nothing to do with Alec and everything to do with her.

"What is it, Carson?" Alec suddenly said. He reached out and tipped her chin up with his hand. "What's wrong?"

She didn't realize a revealing expression had crossed her face, but it must have—at least long enough that a lover would notice.

"What if—?" she started to ask, not quite sure how to phrase what she wanted to say. There wasn't much precedent in her life for this kind of question: *What if you go to jail even though you're innocent?* "What if," she said, taking a deep breath, throwing a napkin on her plate, "things go wrong?"

He smiled to himself. Alec folded his own napkin and deposited it on his own plate. And then he looked up at her.

"We just do what we can do," he said. "There's really nothing else, is there?"

As he lightly brushed her cheek with the back of his hand, she closed her eyes and felt his flesh on hers and tried to commit the sensation to memory.

They spent the rest of the morning wandering through the

softly lit galleries of the British Museum. Carson paid particular attention to paintings that depicted men at war: horses
rearing up, bayonets flashing, soldiers lying splayed and dead
on rain-soaked foreign battlefields. This, too, was flesh: the
potential not for indescribable pleasure but for pain, equally
indescribable. The sheer volume of war imagery in the museum was sufficient to silence the two of them, and she and
Alec barely spoke as they walked through gallery after gallery.
Even if Alec was vindicated in this whole Watchers business,
Carson thought, there was still the prospect of war to think
about. Alec had already told her that he would definitely sign
up to fight the Germans, and she knew, of course, that she
wouldn't try to stop him. The precariousness of life here in
England—this nation so small and vulnerable and close to
Germany—shamed her for a moment, as if she were personally responsible for the easy comforts and certainties of life in
Marlowe, Connecticut, where war was, at most, a bit of un-
pleasantness that might upset a few applecarts on the other
side of the globe.

And yet it was true. She *was* personally responsible, wasn't
she? For herself at least, for her own actions, for her own be-
liefs and convictions and ideals? If not her, then who else?
Who else might possibly be responsible for Carson Weatherell? A generation earlier, of course, the answer would have
been obvious: her parents, or, later, her husband. But this was
1936. Carson had the right to vote now, she had the right to
drink, she had the right to *think*. And to think for *herself*. It
was just as her uncle had told her in his study in Sintra on
that horrible, distant, echoing afternoon—something she
hadn't understood at the time but now, she feared, she under-

stood all too well: Everyone is political. You just have to pick your battles.

And she'd picked hers.

"Where were you?" Alec whispered now, coming up behind her. "You looked far away."

"Yes, about three thousand miles," she answered. "But I'm back now." She reached up over her shoulder to cup his cheek in the palm of her hand, and this time he was the one to close his eyes, as if trying to commit the sensation to memory. "I'm right here," she said.

Later, when they got back to the house, Mrs. Bertram had already returned. She was sitting in the front parlor waiting for them, and the expression on her face was anything but encouraging.

"Sit down, Alec, Carson," she said.

"Did you see Lord Aidan?" Alec burst out before he'd even settled into his chair.

"Yes, yes I did. I will tell you everything."

Mrs. Bertram took a deep breath. Carson reached out from her chair to place a reassuring hand on Alec's arm.

"At first," Mrs. Bertram went on, "he was quite reluctant to say a word. He knew about the case, all right, though he hadn't realized that I knew you. In fact," she said, shifting uncomfortably, "he seemed quite shocked to learn that you had any information about the investigation in the first place. I assured him that I trusted you completely, but he said I was naive. To press his point, he removed a file from a drawer in another office and examined it himself. Your name was on the file, Alec. He wouldn't let me see the contents, but after he'd read them over, he said there was no doubt about your complicity with the Watchers."

"This is madness," said Carson. "We don't even know specifically what the accusation is, or what evidence they have."

"I agree," said Mrs. Bertram. "It *is* madness, and one with an extraordinarily fine pedigree. It's the kind of madness that supposedly democratic and free nations develop when it suits their purposes. On such occasions it can become, shall we say, *difficult* to distinguish between the so-called good guys and the bad guys they're supposedly trying to protect us from. But as much as I'd like to discuss the finer points of this argument, I'm afraid I can't at the moment because, as it happens, we have a far more immediate concern." She turned her attention entirely to Alec now. "It would appear," Mrs. Bertram said, "that the only reason the authorities haven't arrested you yet is that they've wanted to observe your actions and contacts."

"Yes, Carson's already explained that to me," said Alec.

"Well, that situation has changed now," Mrs. Bertram went on. "Given my inquiries, they now know that *you* know. They know that Carson has told you of their suspicions. It used to be that you were more valuable to them as a free man. Now—" She paused, lowering her eyes. "I'm sorry, Alec. I tried."

"Oh, no," Carson gasped.

Alec said nothing. He simply slumped back in his chair, his eyes wide and hollow.

It was the moment they'd both feared for a week now, a possibility they'd discussed and tried to brace themselves for, but in the end nothing could have prepared them for the dull thud of this reality.

"As a good friend of my late husband's," Mrs. Bertram went on, her voice even and quiet, as if she could impose dignity onto the scene through the sheer force of her will, "Lord Aidan did grant me the courtesy of five minutes alone with you first. He didn't have to do that, and I'm grateful to him. When you weren't here earlier, he said they would simply wait outside and return after they'd observed your arrival. And now, my dear Alec, I'm afraid those five minutes—"

But before she could complete her thought there came an insistent, no-nonsense rapping at the front door.

"Carson," Mrs. Bertram said, in the ringing silence that followed, "would you please open the door? I'm afraid I don't quite have it in me."

Carson stood unsteadily. Her legs went liquid for a moment, like that moment on the *Queen Mary* some months earlier when the ship first pushed back from the dock. Another voyage, Carson thought. The beginning of another long journey. Only this time she didn't know where it would lead her, or how long it would take to get wherever it was she was going, if ever.

She opened the door. Four men waited there, and as they brushed past her one of them rattled off the formal introductions—two detectives from the Yard, two from the Ministry of Defence. One of those Defence detectives, however, needed no introduction: Lawrence Emmett. He barely met his niece's gaze as he walked past.

"Lawrence," she tried, "you have to understand why I told Alec—"

"Carson," her uncle said, turning toward her, his face impassive, his lips thin. "You did what you had to do, and now I'm doing what I have to do. Obviously, it was an error on my part to include you in the investigation this summer. We weren't yet ready to bring Mr. Breve here in for questioning, but now we have to. I should never have trusted a young girl with this kind of information, but I didn't know what else to do. I thought you were our best shot."

"I'm not a young girl," Carson said tersely, though the words themselves made her sound young and inexperienced, and she was embarrassed. Still, she didn't know what else to say; she couldn't possibly tell her uncle what she believed: *Love makes you rely on instinct. And sometimes instinct is all you've got.*

Already it was all over. As her uncle had been talking to her, Carson could vaguely hear the murmur of voices from the parlor, the flat declarations of arrest, the mild protestations of innocence, the brusque lockstep footfalls of men on a mission: the other three detectives parading Alec through the foyer.

"Mr. Emmett," Alec managed to say as he was nudged past Lawrence and Carson. "I want you to know that I've done nothing wrong."

Lawrence just nodded impersonally, looking away.

"And Carson—" Alec called back, but it was too late. He was already out the front door, being herded down the steps, alternately turning back to try to catch sight of her and to look down to watch where he was going. A door to a black sedan swung open just long enough to swallow Alec up.

On the tidy, expensive street, there was no commotion, no excitement. A woman walked a small dog, yet she didn't even glance up to see what this official-looking car and all these men were doing in front of Mrs. Bertram's house.

Lawrence, too, was already leaving now, and it took Carson a moment to realize that she had to call after him.

"Can I come with Alec?"

But Lawrence shook his head as he quickly descended the steps. "No," he said over his shoulder. "That wouldn't work." At the sidewalk, he paused and turned, apparently deciding to grant his niece one small comfort. "Don't worry, Carson, nobody is going to hurt him." And then he, too, ducked into the black sedan.

As the car pulled away, Carson caught sight of Alec turning to look at her through the back window. His mouth was forming words, but she couldn't make out what they were. *I love you,* maybe, or *Help me.*

And then what? Alec had asked her that night by the greenhouse back in Connecticut. Carson had laid out a plan that would get them as far as Mrs. Bertram's house in London, and Alec naturally wanted to know where they would go from there. Now Carson was in that house, sipping sherry with Mrs. Bertram and sitting in front of a fire, and the breezy answer she's summoned on the cool autumn night seemed as distant as the town of Marlowe itself: *I'll think of something.*

She'd thought of nothing. The detectives had hustled Alec out of this house hours earlier, and in all that time Carson hadn't been able to think of what she might do to help the situation. At least Mrs. Bertram had known to telephone a barrister she knew named Simon Harkness, who promised to meet Alec at the interview room at the Yard and serve as his legal counsel during the intake. The best Carson had been able to do was root around in the icebox and fix a light supper of roast beef sandwiches for herself and Mrs. Bertram, but the tray of food sat untouched on a table between them.

Carson sat in one wing-backed chair, Mrs. Bertram in its mate. Carson imagined that Mrs. Bertram must have sometimes sat here just like this with her husband, year after year. The night before, Carson and Alec had lain together in bed, their arms and legs entwined; Carson realized now that she was beginning to understand what a marriage would feel like. It was the freedom to sit in front of a fire night after night. It was the freedom to lie with your lover over a period of years, letting time drift past, getting older together yet not really minding, because the years that you mark off are years spent in the company of the one you love.

Carson didn't know if she and Alec would ever have those years. Simon Harkness was a fine lawyer, Mrs. Bertram had assured her, yet the tenor of her words betrayed her own insecurity about Alec's eventual exoneration. Who really had a great deal of sympathy right now for a supposed traitor? The fact was, all Carson could do was what she was doing now: sit still and wait for Simon Harkness to call. But it wasn't enough. Sitting tight and waiting for life to happen to her no longer suited Carson. It no longer satisfied her. It stifled her, frustrated her, made her flush warm all over with pent-up energy.

Or maybe it was the combination of the sherry and the fire that was warming her. Carson placed her empty glass next to the tray on the table. She rubbed her eyes. She looked over at Mrs. Bertram, whose own glass was empty, whose own eyes were closed, whose chin was resting on her chest, whose breaths, Carson felt, leaning her own head back on a wing of her chair, looking affectionately across the room at this elderly woman—whose breaths were pleasingly regular and calm and deep and enviably oblivious.

The telephone rang at nearly midnight. It jolted them both awake. Mrs. Bertram reached for the phone that she'd strung over to the table next to her, fumbled with the heavy receiver, said "Hello."

Carson barely took a breath as she listened to Mrs. Bertram's end of the conversation.

"I see," Mrs. Bertram said. "Yes, of course, I do understand. No, no, Simon, I know. There was nothing you could have— yes, certainly." Then she replaced the receiver with a quiet thud, leaned back in her chair, and sighed deeply. She looked even smaller and frailer than she had before.

"They've formally arrested Alec," she said to Carson. "And they're charging him with treason."

When the sky turned light, Carson put on a coat and slipped out to go for a walk. She couldn't stand to stay inside any longer. Simply walking through the London streets had to be a better idea than sitting stunned in an easy chair in Mrs. Bertram's house. The early morning air was cool, and the pavement was wet and scattered with leaves from the trees that arced overhead.

How beautiful this city was, Carson thought; how peaceful. And yet there was an ominous quality in the air, too, a sense of fragility and temporariness. Or maybe it was just her—the fact that she'd barely slept last night, or that the man she loved was in jeopardy, or that war seemed a certainty, or that she was powerless to do anything about anything.

The roast beef sandwich from the night before had remained untouched, and now Carson stopped for a bite at the pub where she and Alec had eaten breakfast the day before. This time she sat alone in the corner, facing the cracked wall, hunched over the small, scarred table as she chewed a currant scone and drank a cup of strong, unsweetened tea. Out there, somewhere, Alec sat in his own solitary corner. What had happened to him seemed surreal, strange in a way that was reminiscent of *love's* own strangeness, and yet, of course, it was more like love's opposite: isolation instead of union, a flush of sorrow instead of pleasure.

The barman leaned over the bar and asked Carson, "Where's the mister this morning?"

She was startled. They'd been in here only once, yet the barman remembered them. "Oh, he couldn't come with me today," she said, trying to sound casual, taking a small sip from her teacup.

"Too bad, pretty young thing like you, breakfasting all alone, and looking none too happy about it," he said, and he picked up a rag and began wiping down the polished wood of the bar. "It isn't right, no it isn't. Seems like nothing's right with the world these days," he continued to himself. "Everything's out of sorts, and headed for disaster." He yawned softly, then retreated into a room behind the bar.

Carson didn't disagree with his words, and yet, she had to ask herself once again, what was she supposed to *do* about the situation? It was as though she were in the backseat of a car and watching as an accident happened in slow motion. Sitting here in a pub and drinking tea and eating a scone, while elsewhere Alec was being accused of treason, was *crazy*. Although Mrs. Bertram had hired a good barrister to defend Alec, it somehow didn't seem enough. Even if Carson was only going to give the illusion of activity, she wanted to take part in his defense. She didn't know if there was anything she *could* do to help Alec, but she was sure that sitting here crying into her tea wasn't it.

She tossed a few coins onto the table, bade the barman good morning, and then headed out into the street. The sun had come up more fully, and the day was clear. So much for London fog; the white rotunda of the British Museum glowed in the light, and all the surrounding buildings seemed freshly polished, as though the barman from The Rose and Stag had given them a swipe with his rag.

Carson stopped on a sidewalk and tried to get her bearings. During that talk on the lawn with Alec back home in Connecticut, she had vowed to learn to trust herself, and to do so by living moment to moment, step-by-step. And the first step she'd taken that night was toward Alec. Now Carson didn't know where her steps would take her—whether she would somehow stumble toward some possible resolution to the problem of Alec's imprisonment or simply go in circles. All she knew was that she had to take steps, to *walk*, and then to keep walking, as though a destination might appear to her through the simple act of putting one foot in front of the other long enough.

And so, she walked. She passed row houses and tube stations. She passed bookstores and shuttered restaurants. She passed flower shops and fruiterers, and still she walked. She walked along the Thames, she walked among the colonies of pigeons of Trafalgar Square, and she walked past the long row of imposing white marble buildings of Pall Mall. And still she walked, aimlessly yet determined, until finally, when her feet were starting to ache inside the only pair of shoes she'd brought with her to London, she realized where it was she wanted to go, and understood that she wasn't very far away.

Carson's sense of direction had never been very strong, yet somehow she'd seemed to have absorbed bits and pieces of the street map of London during her brief stay there in the summer. So it was that she'd unconsciously wandered toward the vicinity of Claridge's Hotel, where her aunt and uncle lived.

The stone facade of the building was pristine in the early morning light. A doorman in pressed uniform and white gloves—as formal in bearing as a Buckingham Palace beefeater—held open the front door, and Carson walked inside. She thought of her first day in England, earlier that same year, and how she'd arrived at this very hotel, knowing nothing about the world. Frightened. Shy. Out of her element. That first day she'd let her aunt and uncle do most of the talking, and allowed herself the luxury of simply sitting back and basking in the glow of their knowledge and sophistication.

But today, months after that first morning, Carson strode through the lobby of Claridge's with a sense of purpose, even righteousness. She'd trusted Uncle Lawrence, and look what had happened. She needed to confront him face-to-face, to make him talk to her, to force him to reveal more specifics about the case he was helping to build against Alec.

Carson pressed the button on the elevator, and the door slid to one side, folding over itself. She walked into the gilt cage and asked the elevator man to press three, which he did with one gloved finger and a somber nod. As the lift ascended, Carson thought of her uncle's flushed, angry face when he appeared at the doorstep of Mrs. Bertram's yesterday.

If her uncle and Alec were right about war being inevitable, then it was even more urgent to help Alec now. As difficult as it might be to clear Alec under the present turbulent circumstances, after war broke out it would be impossible to find anyone willing to stick his neck out in defense of Alec—Alec the traitor, Alec the German-lover, Alec the "guilty-until-proven-innocent." Not that Carson had any idea what she could possibly say to her uncle to convince him to tell her what kind of evidence the government had collected in its case against Alec. But her intuition, moment to moment, step-by-step, had taken her this far, and now she had to trust herself to do what was next, whatever it was.

"Three, miss," the elevator man was saying.

"Oh. Thank you. Sorry," said Carson, for the elevator doors had been opened for a moment, and she was expected to leave.

Carson stepped onto the pale, deep carpet of Claridge's hallway. She turned and walked along the long corridor toward the door at the far end. When she arrived at Suite 306 she knocked sharply, and then waited.

So: What was it going to be? What would she say? Or, as Alec might ask, "And then what?"

I'll think of something, Carson told herself, and she almost smiled.

"Coming," came a muffled voice from the other side of the door. It wasn't Jane's voice; and it certainly wasn't Lawrence's.

It was a woman's voice, and it might very well have belonged to a hotel maid or to one of Lawrence's secretaries. Yet Carson thought it sounded familiar somehow, though she couldn't quite place it.

There was a fumbling with a latch, and then the turning of a lock. And then the door swung open.

And there standing opposite Carson Weatherell, across the threshold of Suite 306 in Claridge's Hotel, London, England, was her own mother.

CHAPTER TEN

"Carson."

With just one word, Philippa managed to convey equal parts relief at seeing her daughter again and disapproval at what Carson had done. She stepped across the threshold of the hotel suite, opened her arms, and wrapped Carson in a tearful embrace. Carson, stunned, stood still, swaying only to the extent that her mother's attentions demanded.

"Oh, Carson, darling," Philippa said, pulling herself back and gripping Carson by both shoulders, "you've had us all worried sick. Thank God you're all right. Thank God I've found you."

But I didn't want to be found, Carson said to herself. *That was the whole point of my note.* But already her mother had turned and was heading back down the entrance hall into the suite, and Carson had no choice but to follow if she wanted to see Lawrence. She turned a corner and entered the drawing room, where she found Jane waiting, standing at the far end, arms crossed, posture straight, and Carson somehow sensed that her aunt and her mother had been having an argument. Jane, seeing who the visitor was, unfolded her arms now and smiled and crossed to Carson, giving her niece a kiss on both cheeks. "Carson," she said. "This *is* a pleasant surprise."

"Well, this isn't," Carson said, gesturing toward Philippa. "Mother," she said, "what *are* you doing here?"

"Well," her mother began, easing herself onto the couch and patting the cushion next to her, indicating that Carson should sit there, "it wasn't easy, let me tell you. When we found that awful note of yours, it gave us quite a fright, as you can imagine. Your father and I simply had no idea what to do. At first we thought that surely you would come to your senses and telephone us. But then, when you didn't, I had a hunch this disappearing act of yours might have something to do with that man Jane had written me about during the summer, the one who'd been sending you all those letters. And that's when I thought to telephone Jane."

"It was Lawrie who knew your exact whereabouts, actually," Jane spoke up, seating herself in the chair opposite Carson and Philippa, the same one where Carson had sat on her first day in London. "When he got home from work that day, I told him about Philippa's call. He seemed hesitant at first, and then he made me promise not to ask him how or why he knew, but in the end he said I could ring Philippa back and tell her that Carson was on board a ship that had just sailed from New York for Southampton. He also said I was to instruct Philippa that she was not to interfere. No cables to the ship, for instance. Matters were to be allowed to 'run their course,' was how he put it. It was all very mysterious, especially as it concerned you and Alec, but one learns not to ask questions after a while, when one is married to someone in British intelligence."

"So," Philippa said, "I simply booked passage on the next available transatlantic crossing, as you might imagine."

"No, actually, I *can't* imagine," said Carson. "Why would you need to come all the way here?"

"Why, to make sure you were safe, Carson darling."

"But you could have simply asked Jane to do that."

"Yes, well," Jane herself said, reaching down to the silver service on the table and pouring coffee into a fresh cup. "My sister doesn't exactly approve of my influence on you, as I've been hearing from her this morning. You take your coffee black, as I recall," she went on, nudging the cup and saucer across the table toward Carson.

"All I know," Philippa said, "is that when Carson left for Europe this summer she was a cheerful, outgoing young woman with a full social calendar and her pick of the eligible well-to-do young men in Marlowe, and when she came back she was a morose, moody homebody with some sort of fixation on, well, I'm not sure what."

"She'd fallen in love, Philippa," said Jane. "What was I to do—deny her one of life's greatest pleasures and mysteries?"

"*Love,*" Philippa repeated, adding a mildly derisive timbre to the word. "This wasn't love. This was . . . I don't know what. Infatuation. Obsession. Sorry, dear," she went on, turning to Carson, planting a hand on her knee, "but you can't blame me for saying what I think."

"You wouldn't be saying any of this if you saw what I saw this summer," Jane said to Philippa, then turned to Carson. "The way you and Alec behaved around each other—my God, it was like looking at myself and Lawrie about a million years ago, back when we decided to get married."

"Carson is hardly old enough to be entrusted with making such decisions," said Philippa.

"Why, she's the same age I was when I met Lawrie," said Jane.

"As I say," said Philippa, and Jane stiffened as if she'd been slapped.

"Enough!" said Carson. She had to wonder what exactly was going on here. Somehow this morning she'd found her way to the hotel without really knowing where she was heading; then once she'd gotten here, she realized exactly what she wanted: information from her uncle. What she'd gotten instead was her mother and aunt in midargument—an argument, moreover, that at first impression might seem to be about *her*, as if she were some sort of trophy, but that actually centered around, Carson suspected, some ancient rivalry between the two sisters. *That's* what got her mother on a transatlantic ship, Carson thought: not her daughter; her sister. "Look," Carson said now, "I haven't come back to England just because I love Alec. And I *do* love Alec," she emphasized for the benefit of her mother, who simply pursed her lips and looked in the other direction. "But there's something far more important going on here, and I really must speak to Lawrence about it."

"In that case I'm afraid you've just missed him," Jane answered. "He's gone to the office."

"Oh, no." Carson fell back against the couch cushion.

"He left rather early for him—I suspect when he saw where my conversation with Philippa was headed," Jane said. "Is there anything I can help you with?"

"No," Carson said, her voice empty of emotion. Then,

after a moment, she added, "You really don't know what I'm talking about? What's going on here? Why I've come all this way back to England?"

Her aunt shook her head. "As I said, Lawrie tells me little about his work. Nothing, is more like it. And I do take it that this has something to do with his work, though I can't imagine how."

Carson nodded numbly. She was already thinking of how she would have to track Lawrence down at his office, and as unlikely as prying information out of him here at home might have been, even if Jane had helped, it seemed ridiculous to hope to do so at the ministry itself.

Carson looked up at her aunt. Jane was looking back at her, eagerly, ready to assist as always. Carson thought of that moment on the train during the return trip to Paris, when Jane had offered to be Carson's confidante, and Carson had declined out of some sense of loyalty to Lawrence. But where had that loyalty gotten her? Where had her loyalty to Lawrence gotten *Alec*? And then Carson thought about how she'd told Jane on the train that one day she *would* confide in her.

That day had come, Carson decided.

She didn't see how telling Alec's story to her aunt, let alone her mother, might help, but neither did she see what else she could do. Anyway, who knew? Maybe it *would* help in some way she couldn't anticipate.

"Look," Carson said, "what I'm about to tell you—well, it's something I probably *shouldn't* be telling you. But I don't see any other way out right now."

"Oh, don't be so melodramatic, Carson," said her mother.

But already Carson was gathering herself. She closed her eyes, took a deep breath, then launched into the story of Alec and the Watchers. She began in Lawrence's study on that afternoon in Sintra and the role she'd been asked to play with Alec over the following three days, continued back in the States with the letters she'd received from Alec as well as his midnight visit to Marlowe, and concluded with the events of the past forty-eight hours, ever since she and Alec had appeared on Mrs. Bertram's doorstep and right up through Carson's arrival at Claridge's and what she'd hoped to ask Lawrence.

When she was done, Philippa blinked at her several times, as if Carson had suddenly popped into the room from another planet. Finally, rather blankly, she said—and it was equally a statement and a question: "So my daughter is a spy?"

But it was Jane who let out a small gasp, and then another, and then said, "Oh, my poor girl. My poor, poor girl." Jane got up from her chair and crossed to Carson, squeezing beside her on the couch and wrapping her arms around her niece. Carson leaned into her, resting her head on Jane's shoulder, hugging her aunt back. After a moment, though, she felt Jane's mouth moving at her ear. "Lawrence couldn't have known what he was asking of you," her aunt whispered. "In Portugal, those last three days. With Alec. *You* know what I mean."

Carson pulled back and looked at her aunt. "You knew?"

"Knew what?" said her mother, but Jane was speaking only to Carson now.

"As I said," Jane said, "you reminded me of Lawrie and myself. The way you prepared for him, getting dressed, trying to look a certain way. And then the way you seemed whenever

you returned to Sintra from an afternoon in Lisbon. How"—
a darting glance here past Carson to Philippa, then back to
Carson—"*worldly* you were. My God," she went on, "I can't
imagine what it was like for you those final days there, thinking what you thought about Alec, but having to, to, to . . .
pretend to love him anyway."

Carson closed her eyes, not so much to ward off the pain
of the memory as to compose herself. Her aunt knew about
the full nature of her relationship with Alec, had known all
along, had done nothing to interfere. Had approved, perhaps.

Carson lowered her aunt's arms from her own shoulders,
took her aunt's hands into her own, and gave them a squeeze.
"The thing is," she said, "despite everything Uncle Lawrence
says, I believe Alec now. I know," she hurried on, "it must
sound foolish. Crazy."

"Not to me—" Jane began.

"Well, it does to me," Philippa interrupted.

"—but I don't know what I could possibly do to help you,"
Jane went on. "I can't just go up to Lawrie when he comes
home from the office tonight and ask him what evidence they
have regarding Alec. First, he'd never give it to me, and second, it wouldn't exactly improve his estimation of you if he
knew you'd told me. Told *us*," she added, looking past Carson
again to Philippa. "*Two* people who have no business knowing. Unless . . ."

Jane turned her face away from Carson and, after a moment, slowly stood up. Carson craned forward slightly.

"Unless?" she said.

"There is one possibility," her aunt said. "No, I couldn't."

"Couldn't . . . what?" Carson prompted.

"It's out of the question, I'm afraid," Jane said, crossing back to her chair.

"What is?" said Carson.

"Now that I think about it, I don't even understand what good this information you want from Lawrence would do you anyway. How would knowing what evidence they have against Alec help?"

Carson shook her head. "I don't know. I can't say. Maybe it *wouldn't* help. But it would be *something*, wouldn't it, Jane? It would be information, which is more than I have now. I can believe in Alec all I want, but the faith of a foolish young girl isn't going to mean much to the authorities."

"So you're out to prove Alec's innocence? That's a rather tall order."

"I don't know what I'm out to do," Carson said miserably, running a hand through her hair. "But I do know this: These last few days I've learned to trust myself, or tried to, anyway. I've learned to follow my intuition. And my intuition right now is telling me that at the very least I should know *why* Alec is in prison."

Jane stood quite still. Her arms were folded in front of her, and her posture was rigid; she looked just as she had when Carson entered the room this morning, though this time the argument she seemed to be having wasn't with Philippa but with herself. A full minute passed while Jane stood absolutely still and gazed off toward a window. Outside, the branches of a tree moved slightly. They were mostly bare, and their bareness somehow looked more white than brown in the glare of the morning sun. Every so often a car horn sounded. A whistle shrilled; the beefeaterlike hotel doorman must be calling for a taxicab. Finally Jane returned her gaze to Carson.

"I can't," she said. "I'm sorry, Carson. Truly I am. Lawrence trusts me, and I would never do anything to betray that trust. I do hope you understand. You must. Lawrie and I—well, we trust each other the way you and Alec trust each other."

Carson was silent, considering this. "If that's true," she then said calmly, "surely he trusts you to do what *you* think is right."

At this, Jane straightened even more, if possible, and her eyes narrowed at Carson. Her aunt, Carson thought, was regarding her with a new appreciation, though what she might conclude from this fresh analysis was anybody's guess. But then Jane allowed herself a slight smile, gave her head a little shake, and turned to her sister.

"This young generation, Philippa," she said. "What *are* we going to do with them? You. Come," she added to Carson.

Carson hopped off the couch and followed her aunt down a hall and into the bedroom area of the suite. Off the master bedroom was a smaller room that had a desk and bookshelves. This, Cason supposed, was Lawrence's study. Without pausing, Jane opened his desk drawers one by one. "Now, let's see, where does he keep this old thing?" she muttered to herself.

"What old thing?" asked Carson.

"His journal," said Jane.

"What?" said Carson. "We can't read his journal."

"Oh, come on, you're going to get cold feet on me now?" said Jane. "You give me this whole sob story about how you know Alec is innocent, and then you want to back out?"

"I didn't say that," said Carson.

"Besides," she said, "*you're* the spy." Suddenly she stopped. "Hullo," Jane said to herself. She'd uprooted a slender black leather-bound book out of the bottom drawer. "Of course," she said, "I can't be certain he's even written about Alec, but if he has, it will be the truth. Lawrence is a great believer in journals. He's been keeping them since he was a boy at Eton." She flipped through the pages quickly until she found an entry that gave her pause.

"Ah, here we are," she said quietly, and she glanced quickly down the page. Carson had come around behind the desk, but Jane now raised the journal so that all her niece could see was its outside covers. "I think I should read what Lawrie has to say first," Jane said. "If it doesn't involve Alec, there's no need for you to be invading my husband's privacy, too."

"Of course," Carson said, but as she stood back and let Jane read the page, she couldn't help studying her aunt's face, scouring it for some telltale response.

And she got it. When Jane had finished reading and looked up from the book, her eyes were wide and watery. Apologetic, even. "I'm sorry," she said as she turned the journal around and handed it to Carson. "I'm so sorry."

Her hands shaking, Carson took the journal, smoothed an already smooth page with one hand, and then, halfway down, found the relevant entry. The blood was pounding so hard behind her eyes that at first she could barely focus. But she forced herself to continue. It was the truth she wanted, and it was the truth she would get.

"Monday P.M.," Lawrence had written in his formal handwriting.

Devastating development today. Home Office cabled with identity of Cambridge informer attending Lisbon conference: none other than our own A.B.—"our own" because, as Carson's boyfriend, he has become almost family. Good lad, thought even I. But evidence is overwhelming: copy of textbook, Dynamics of Radio Telegraphy and Encryption, *with A.B.'s signature on flyleaf (handwriting analysis confirms as his), pertinent passages underlined; worse, a ring with German insignia . . . and "To Alec" engraved on inside. Both apparently "donated" as proof of loyalty. Discovered, after recent Watchers meeting, during secret infiltration of home of MP Alistair Grant. Items photographed on site; left there so as not to arouse suspicion among Watchers.*

All of which presents terrible complications re Carson. Personal, professional. Think I've found solution, though—get her to stay close to A. She'll know truth about him; he won't suspect about us. Nothing else for it, really. Only three more days. Still, awfully difficult to break news to her, poor thing. She has been the pleasant surprise of summer. Bright, beautiful, resourceful. Is she up to this? Don't know. Only know I

Carson had reached the end of the page, but as she turned to the next page Jane took the journal back out of her hands.

"Really, I should look first," Jane said. She glanced down, turned the page. This time, Carson wasn't trying to read the response in her aunt's face. Still, she thought she noticed something flicker there.

"What is it?" Carson said. "There's more? I don't know if I can take it."

"No," Jane said, blinking, looking up. "Nothing involving you, anyway." And she snapped the journal shut and dropped it back into the bottom drawer. Then she turned to Carson, wrapped an arm around her shoulders, and said, "You look like you could use some tea."

She helped Carson back to the drawing room, escorted her onto the couch next to Philippa, and poured her a cup of tea. Then she poured a cup of tea for herself. Jane stood sipping it, putting the cup back on the saucer in her other hand, then sipping some more. As she did so, she regarded Carson, as if to assess her reaction to what had just happened.

"What is it?" Philippa said. "What's wrong? Carson? Jane? Won't someone tell me?"

Carson, however, turned her face up so as to address her aunt directly. "I still believe him," she said.

"Oh, Carson—" her aunt began.

"There's been a horrible mistake. That's all. A cock-up. Isn't that what you call it over here?"

"Carson, please," Jane said. She placed the cup and saucer on the table and crouched before Carson. "You must listen to reason. There's evidence. There's that book, and that awful ring—"

"It's only inscribed to 'Alec.' Surely there are other Alecs in Great Britain," Carson said, but even as she was saying this, she heard how hollow it sounded. "I don't know. I don't *know*. I don't know *anything*. Maybe you're right. Maybe you're all right, you and Lawrence and you," she said, turning to her mother. Then she covered her face with both hands; and then she removed them. She shook them in front of herself, as if trying to get a grip on something enormous. "But what else can I do? I've got to believe Alec. If I don't, who will?"

"Now, Carson," Jane said, taking Carson's shaking hands in her own and then giving them a good squeeze, just as Carson had done for her earlier, "I want you to listen to me. I'm as great an advocate as you'll ever find when it comes to following one's heart. It's what I did in 1917 when I met Lawrie. There I was, hopelessly besotted with this rather peculiar and shy British officer I'd met in the lobby of a movie theater in London who was over there on some secret diplomatic mission. I wanted nothing more than to stay in England with him. Yes, he'd soon be going off to the front, and of course he could never support me in the style to which I was accustomed. But the most important thing, and I know that it will be difficult for you to believe this today, that it will sound rather quaint and old-fashioned, but the most compelling argument against my running off with him was that it *just wasn't done*. Everyone said so. My mother and father. My friends. My own sister," and she reached out and grasped Philippa's hand now in addition to Carson's. For the first time all morning, Carson saw Jane grant her sister a smile, however bittersweet. "And I daresay ten out of ten people I might have stopped on the street would have said so, too," Jane went on. "And do you know what? I didn't listen to any of them. I did what no young woman, no mere girl, did in those days. I did what I wanted. I stayed in England and waited for Lawrie. I followed my *heart*. Because I *knew* him," and she gave Carson's hand a significant squeeze, to let Carson know that the nature of her relationship with Lawrence had been on the same level of intimacy as Carson's with Alec: that they had been lovers. "But *you*, darling girl, darling, darling Carson," Jane went on, letting go of Carson's hand to reach up and brush the hair off her niece's forehead, to tuck it behind her ear, to stroke the side of her face, "you must understand that sometimes you have to listen to your head, too."

Carson looked into her aunt's tender, loving face, and she felt for a moment as if she might cry. So she looked at her own hands, folded in her lap.

She heard her mother say, "Thank you, Jane. That was very thoughtful of you."

She heard the creak of Jane's knees as she raised herself from a crouching to a standing position.

She heard the sniffling of her aunt to one side of her and of her mother to the other.

And then she heard silence.

They were waiting for her.

Carson stood. She was nodding her head, composing her thoughts, as she crossed the room. When she reached the hallway of the suite, she turned back to her aunt and her mother, two sisters still fighting a battle from a time before she herself was born.

"Thank you," she said in a voice that seemed too soft to have carried very far. So she cleared her throat and tried again. "Thank you. Both of you. I do hope you understand. But I have to do what I have to do."

"And what is that?" Jane said.

Carson smiled, and she realized it was the same bittersweet smile her aunt had given her mother several minutes earlier.

"I'll think of something," she said.

And why not? Carson said to herself as she descended in the lift. The strategy of relying on her intuition—of trusting herself to think of something, of going with her gut, as they might have said back in the States—had worked so far. Not in the ways she'd thought it would; walking up to the door of Jane and Lawrence's suite, for instance, she couldn't possibly have known she was about to be reunited with her own mother. Still, it had worked: Carson was walking away from there now with precisely the information she'd come to get.

The problem, of course, was the information itself: the evidence against Alec. As she left the lobby of Claridge's and fully reentered a world of trilling whistles and argumentative automobile horns, Carson couldn't help reflecting on the contrast between her aunt's description of what she had wanted out of her courtship with Lawrence long ago and what Carson was hoping to accomplish now. Back then, Jane had been acting out of a personal conviction, taking the kind of social stand that might seem ahead of its time, even brave. You might resent her for it, as the members of her own family had; but you also had to respect her for it, even if you couldn't admit it to yourself. Carson, by contrast, knew how her own actions must appear to her mother and her aunt—as stubbornness, a willful effort to ignore the evidence.

But just the opposite was true. Carson wasn't ignoring the evidence at all. Now that she knew what the evidence against Alec was, maybe she could do something about it. That had been her intention all along, even if she hadn't known exactly what it was she would be able to do with the information once she had it. But now she did.

She would go to Cambridge. The book and the ring were meaningless to her—and yes, she was willing to admit now that somehow they must have belonged to Alec—but maybe they wouldn't be meaningless to Alec's closest friends. Carson, after all, had known Alec for barely three months, and much of that time she'd spent ignoring him. Tom and Michael and Freddy, however, had known Alec for years. If anyone other than Alec himself could clear up the mystery of the book and the ring—and visiting the defendant in a case as sensitive as this one would be impossible, Simon Harkness had emphatically informed Carson—it would have to be his closest friends.

The train trip to Cambridge was picturesque, Carson supposed, though she barely noticed the sights. Still, when the train pulled into the station, she couldn't miss the majesty of the city, the power that seemed to reside in the spires and towers of these academic fortresses. She'd never been much of a student before, always preferring to chat with her friends instead of truly learning with the kind of depth that real scholars did. But now, for a moment, she felt a pang of longing, wishing she could settle here and learn everything there was to learn—with Alec at her side, of course.

Walking up the winding streets of Cambridge, Carson consulted the street map she'd bought for ten pence at the train station and made her way to the row house where Alec and his colleagues shared a flat. The bell made a buzzing sound when she pressed it, and within a moment Michael Morling appeared in the doorway.

"Carson?" he said, seeming genuinely amazed that she was standing there. "I thought Alec went to the States to see *you*. What's going on?"

"Long story," said Carson quietly. "May I come in?"

"Of course," said Michael, and he stepped aside so that

Carson could pass. She entered the narrow front hall, with its smells of cooked beef and tinned beans, and walked past a small sitting room with old brown furniture and dull ocher-colored walls. She was just about to wonder why in the world these men chose to live here when she entered the living room, an enormous, welcoming space filled with books and light. This was more like it. Here, she could imagine Alec making himself right at home. It was just as Alec had described it to her: the beautiful mess of an orderly mind.

Carson turned to Michael and pointed vaguely down another hall. "Which is Alec's?" she said.

"First door there," he said. He pointed the way, but he didn't follow Carson. He let her do the exploring on her own.

Alec's bedroom was small and tidy and, again, exactly as he'd described it. Warm prints on the walls, desk cluttered with papers, bed unmade—she half expected Alec to be sleeping in it. Carson lightly touched his pillow, running her hand along its smooth surface as though it were Alec's face. She closed her eyes, remembering that moment in the pub with Alec the previous day, when she'd tried to commit the sensation of his hand on her cheek to memory. Then she turned and went back out into the living room, where Michael, Tom, and Freddy were now assembled.

"Hello, Carson," Tom said. "What's wrong? You look worried."

"Where's Alec?" said Freddy.

"I *am* worried," said Carson. "About Alec. He's been arrested."

"Arrested?" said Tom. "For what?"

"Treason," Carson said simply.

The three men gaped at her. Michael emitted a little laugh. "You're putting us on," he said.

But Carson's expression told them everything they needed to know.

"You're *not* putting us on," Michael said, sinking into a chair.

"I don't *believe* it," said Tom.

"Good *Lord*," Freddy echoed.

"I mean," said Michael, "it's absurd. It's ridiculous. Alec isn't a *traitor*."

"Well, the government thinks he is," said Carson, and for a moment she heard Lawrence's gentle, admonishing voice, telling her to confide in no one, but already she'd told her aunt, and she'd told her mother, and Mrs. Bertram knew, and where exactly was the harm? So she plunged ahead. "They say he's a member of the Watchers, and that he's been passing technical information to the Germans. And he's in a terrible mess right now, and I thought maybe if I came here and talked to his dearest friends, you might be able to tell me something, I don't know what, but *something* that would help, that could make a difference somehow. Because that's all I've got right now, this hope, this *faith*—this faith in Alec, this faith that something will happen. Because that's what's been going on lately. I've just been putting one foot in front of the other and somehow getting where I'm going without even knowing I wanted to go there, and that's what I was hoping would happen now, here, by coming to Cambridge and seeing you. That, I don't know, that I would find something, or that one of you would tell me something."

She was beginning to lose it. She could hear it for herself, in the tumbling-out shapelessness of her words and thoughts. She could see it for herself, reflected back at her in the three puzzled, perhaps alarmed, faces bunched before her.

"I guess," she said, "I just stupidly trusted that I would think of something."

And then she did.

These moments don't come often in life. It had happened to Carson only once before, on the train to Lisbon, when she stood on the rear platform and realized that her life had reached a now-or-never turning point, and she had decided: now. Twice, maybe, if she counted that moment this morning when she had told her aunt that the trust of a lover means trusting yourself to do what *you* think is right. But it definitely was happening again here, in this humble sitting room in Cambridge. What she was experiencing was a moment of stunning clarity. It was a moment of perfect conviction. It was the moment that everything else has been leading up to, without you knowing it—but then when you do know it, there's no doubt that *this is it.*

"The police," Carson said now, looking at the three promising young men grouped before her, "found a photograph and a ring."

Her uncle had said that British intelligence had known for some time that someone from Cambridge was slipping information to the Germans. It wasn't Alec; Carson still believed that. But what if it was one of the three men in this room with her? It might not be. But then again, it might. There was one way to find out, and all of a sudden she'd known what it was.

It was Freddy who took the bait.

"It wasn't a pho—" he began, then stopped himself.

"Wasn't a what, Freddy?" Carson said. "A photograph? No, it wasn't. You're right about that. But how could you possibly know that? Yet you do. So you must know that it was actually a *book* and a ring. And I'll bet you know what book it was, too, don't you, Freddy? It was a book that you found here among poor Alec's boxes."

"Now, hold on," Freddy said.

"What's going on here, Freddy?" said Tom.

"Nothing's going on," Freddy said. He tried a laugh. "It's just a misunderstanding."

"No," said Michael, standing up. "I don't think so. I think you know more than you're saying."

There was an agonizing moment of silence, in which Carson and the two men regarded Freddy Hunt. And in that moment of taking stock, they all knew.

Freddy took a step back. "Jesus, don't keep *staring* at me, all of you," he said. "I'm just *me*, all right? Same person you've always known. Kid from Yorkshire, remember?"

"I think maybe I've never known who you are," said Tom quietly.

"I'm someone with ambitions, all right?" said Freddy. "A desire to be more than some second-rate academic holed up in a tutorial for the rest of my life. I mean, face it, what good are either of you ever going to accomplish? How are you ever going to do, really *do*, anything with your lectures and your papers? Mike, Tom, who gives a damn about you and your 'contributions to society'? The future isn't in the decrepit halls of the *academy*, it's in the battlefield, and in the strategy room. It's taking place among the decision makers. The men who count. Men like Alistair Grant and the other Watchers. Men who will lead us through the century."

There was silence. Then Carson said, "But why *Alec?*"

"Because he's *perfect*," said Freddy. "Maybe not dirt-poor like me. But from a poor enough background so the government should have no trouble drumming up a case that he's full of bitterness and resentments against foreigners and Hebrews."

"As full of bitterness as you," said Michael.

"Oh, please," said Freddy. "You're the ones who should be bitter. Unlike the two of you, I've actually got a promising future. You see, the Watchers appreciate my mind. They need a theoretical physicist among them. They appreciate me more than anyone at dear old Cambridge. The Watchers want to know what I think, and I tell them. And I'm going to tell them plenty more, believe me. I know quite a lot about telegraphy. There's a tutorial I plan to give. And they're all going to attend. I met a German, Heinz Boller, who wants me to come to Munich to talk to some scientists there."

While he'd been saying all this, Freddy had also been inching backward, toward the front hall. Now he suddenly turned and ran, and in a moment they heard the front door banging open. Michael and Tom immediately went after him, but Freddy was small and fast, and Carson suspected they'd never catch up.

Aunt Jane and Uncle Lawrence's suite at Claridge's was festooned once again with ribbons and a banner, just as it had been when Carson arrived in London three months earlier, only this time the sign read WELCOME, ALEC. And this time there were three trays of small, carefully constructed hors d'oeuvres, not one tray, as well as three silver buckets of champagne on ice.

Jane was there, of course. So was Philippa. Michael and Tom gathered around the chair where Mrs. Bertram sat, saying how lovely it was to finally meet the woman who meant so much to Alec, and how each of them wished he had a Mrs. Bertram in his life, and how everyone should have a Mrs. Bertram in his or her life. "Well, that's all very well," Mrs. Bertram answered them. "But then who should I have in *my* life?"

The room erupted in laughter, but this noise was nothing compared with the roar that greeted Alec a moment later when he walked into the room, followed by Carson and Lawrence. Carson, Michael, and Tom had called on Lawrence at his office the same afternoon that Carson had visited Cambridge, and if at first Lawrence was aghast that Carson had confided details of Alec's case to yet two more people, even he had to admit the story they told about what had happened that very afternoon made for pretty compelling evidence that Freddy had framed Alec with items he'd found among Alec's belongings in Cambridge. Lawrence excused himself to consult with his superiors. He returned to his office more than an hour later and, while Carson, Michael, and Tom watched him anxiously, calmly picked up the receiver of his telephone, dialed, and after a moment said, "Jane, I think a celebration would be in order this evening."

And so Michael and Tom went to Claridge's to await the triumphant return of Alec, while Lawrence led Carson into a sub-subbasement of London Prison. It would have been dark outside by now, Carson realized, though here inside this windowless netherland where Alec had spent the past thirty-six hours, time wasn't measured in increments of days and nights. It simply went by, unmeasured, somehow endured.

When the policemen brought Alec out of the cell, he looked frailer than when she'd seen him last, and frightened. He let her hold him, though at first he seemed merely stunned and unresponsive. He wore prisoner's grays, and he hadn't shaved, so his face seemed etched in charcoal. Still, as Carson kissed him and cried and spoke softly to him, he started to come around, like someone being awakened from a terrible dream.

"They're really letting me go?" he asked in a voice that sounded somehow rusted.

"Yes, Alec, they are. I promise. It's all over."

And it was, in a way. Alec closed his eyes and kissed Carson's face, her cheek, her mouth, and within moments her own tears were mixed with his, and she didn't know who was crying harder. Then Lawrence made a throat-clearing noise, and Alec walked with Carson upstairs to sign some papers and collect his possessions and change his clothes, and then the three of them rode in a taxi to Claridge's. There, in Suite 306, Alec slowly worked his way around the room, hugging and kissing everyone, until he got to the one person he didn't know.

"Well, now that I've gotten to meet Mrs. Bertram," Carson said, wrapping her arm through Alec's, "I thought it only fair that you meet my mother."

Alec looked at Carson, then at Philippa, then at Carson again, as if to make sure she wasn't kidding. Carson hadn't

prepared Alec for this moment. But then, Carson hadn't prepared *herself* for this moment. She'd thought about it in the
taxi on the way over, but she had decided that there simply
was no way to anticipate what might happen. And so, as she
had learned to do over these last few days, Carson had decided to just let whatever happened . . . happen.

"Mrs. Weatherell," Alec said, when he'd recovered, reaching out to the woman on the couch. "It's a pleasure."

"Please," she answered, receiving his handshake, "call me
Philippa. And who knows?" she added, with an eye toward
her daughter. "Maybe one day you'll even be able to call me
Mother. After all, any man who inspires such faith in my
daughter must be special."

It was that kind of evening all around. Alec turned out to
have a perfectly good explanation of how a German ring with
his name inscribed along the inner band had come into his
possession. His father, it seems, had found it in the last war,
pocketing it on a battlefield and sending it home to his wife,
with a note instructing her to sell it if money got tight. But
even before the ring reached her, Alec's father was killed. The
ring, Alec's mother told him years later, when she presented
it to him on his sixteenth birthday, would always show that
his father had been there in the Great War, fighting the good
fight. Alec sighed now, then added that if he'd known what
the supposedly treasonous evidence against him was, he
would have been able to offer the detectives this explanation.
At this, Lawrence made a sour face and allowed as to how,
well, yes, certain methods of interrogation and investigation
might indeed be improved, and everyone else in the room
hissed at first, as if Lawrence were a movie villain, but then

they broke up laughing. Then Alec toasted Lawrence for being big enough to admit his errors, and then Lawrence toasted Alec for being big enough to forgive what he might reasonably have considered unforgivable, and then everyone toasted Alec and Carson for having seen each other through this ordeal, and then Carson said she wanted to propose a toast, and everyone knew from the tone of her voice that it was going to be serious and heartfelt, and the room grew silent.

"To the two most precious things in the world," Carson said, raising her glass, as a simple bracelet with blue beads slipped down her wrist. "Friends and family."

And so there the story might have ended: Alec a free man, Lawrence a humbled civil servant, Philippa a forgiving mother, and finally, Carson in love with not only the prince she wanted, but one of whom her mother actually approved. Happily ever after, and all that.

If only Carson hadn't been bothered by something. It had been nagging at her all day, ever since the morning, but she'd had to put it out of her mind so as to pursue the information about Alec, first all the way to Alec's flat in Cambridge, then back to her uncle's office in London. But now, as the evening wore on, and the three trayfuls of appetizers shrank down to crumbs, and one, then two, then three empty bottles were placed bottoms-up back into their buckets, where they bobbed in the water from the melting ice, Carson decided that the time had come to find out. That's what she did these days, wasn't it? Take one step, then another, until she reached the truth. And so, when she hoped nobody was looking, Carson removed herself from the drawing room, sought out the master-bedroom suite, and entered the little room off to the side, where she reached into the desk's bottom drawer and produced a leather-bound book.

Her aunt had seemed eager for Carson not to see what Lawrence had written on the page after the entry Carson *had* been allowed to read. Jane might have simply been protecting her husband's privacy, of course, and no doubt to some degree she was. But Carson couldn't shake the suspicion that her aunt had read something else there, something involving Carson. When they'd walked into the room that morning, Carson had been concerned that the journal might reveal something about Alec; her aunt had shared her concern. And their shared concern had been proven well founded as to the likelihood of his guilt, at least as far as they knew at that time. Surely if her aunt, reading the following page, had wanted to reassure Carson, she would have confirmed that it contained nothing involving Alec. But what she'd said instead to Carson was this: *Nothing involving you*—leading Carson to wonder if precisely the opposite was true: that it did indeed involve her.

She found where she'd left off:

Still, awfully difficult to break news to her, poor thing. She has been the pleasant surprise of summer. Bright, beautiful, resourceful. Is she up to this? Don't know. Only know I

Carson turned the page.

love her as I would a daughter. Sigh. This whole business damn confusing. If only we could tell her who she really is.

"Carson!" Her uncle's booming voice made her jump. She slammed the book shut with a bang like a gunshot and looked up and saw him standing in the doorway to the bedroom suite. "I can't believe this," he fairly shouted, and he quickly advanced on her, holding out one hand for the offending object.

" 'If only we could tell her who she really is,' " Carson recited from memory.

This was sufficient to stop her uncle in his tracks.

"What?" he said.

"So, who am I, really?" she said.

"I'm sure I—I mean, I—I should—"

But he was spared further stammering by the appearance in the doorway behind him of first Jane and then Philippa. "What's all this yelling and banging about?" Jane said, but then she saw the book in Carson's hands.

" 'If only we could tell her who she really is,' " Carson repeated evenly, holding the journal out in front of her, pointing it at her uncle. "So *who am I?*"

Lawrence turned helplessly to his wife. Jane in turn shook her head, equally helplessly, then turned beseechingly to her sister. Philippa in turn looked at Jane, looked at Lawrence, took a deep breath, and then walked past both of them. When she reached Carson, she held out both her hands. Carson tucked the journal tight against herself at first, thinking it was what Philippa wanted. But then she realized that Philippa wanted *her*. So, slowly, she set the book on the desk and reached back. She took Philippa's hands and looked her in the eye. And then she waited for what she already knew was coming.

"Jane and Lawrence are your parents," Philippa said.

"Philippa!" Jane cried.

"It's true," Philippa said calmly. "It's no use keeping it a secret anymore. I think Carson is ready for the truth, as confusing and difficult and even, I'm afraid, as painful as it may be. I wouldn't have dared to believe she was ready until I saw it for myself this morning. The two of you—Carson, Jane—the two of you had *discovered* each other this summer. You had more to say to each other now than either of you had to say to me. I wouldn't have pursued this matter on my own, mind you. I wouldn't have chosen to make this particular truth known. But now that this moment is here, this *truth* is here, I think you're ready for it, don't you, dear?"

Carson nodded weakly. She didn't know if she believed what Philippa was saying, that she could handle this particular revelation. But it did make sense, in a way. The tension between the sisters. The long-standing distrust of Lawrence. Everything, in fact, that had to do with the aunt and uncle whom Carson had grown up knowing only as distant figures across the Atlantic. But now she *was* grown up, and it was just as her mother said: Given half a chance, Jane had become Carson's confidante.

"Carson," Jane was saying, "please, please forgive me. Forgive us," and she reached out for Lawrence's hand and pulled her husband close. Lawrence, for his part, said, "Carson, you must believe us, we did try to do what was best—" but Carson cut him off.

"There's nothing to forgive. I understand. Or I think I do, anyway. You weren't married at the time, Jane, but your sister was."

"And your father—my husband—and I couldn't have children, as it turned out," said Philippa. "That was quite a blow."

"So it was all rather convenient," said Carson.

"Perhaps too much so," said Jane.

But Carson was shaking her head. "No, I won't hear of it, Jane. You wanted more out of life than a child and a safe haven in Connecticut. You wanted to *live*."

"Yes," said Jane softly.

"But," Carson said to her mother, "you wanted to live, too. And for you, to live—to really and truly live—was to raise a child."

Her mother nodded.

"What's going on here?" It was Alec, poking his head in the room. "Everyone's going home out there. Making apologies. Tom and Michael have to catch the last train to Cambridge, and Mrs. Bertram's tired—"

But then he sensed the mood of the room and stopped himself.

"Say," he said, "what *is* going on here?"

"Just the end of a story that we'll tell our children, and our grandchildren, and maybe, if we're lucky, they'll tell *their* children and grandchildren," said Carson. "And do you know what the best part is?"

Alec shook his head no. Carson turned to Jane and Lawrence.

"Do you?" Carson said. "Know what the best part is?"

They shook their heads, too.

"*You* do," Carson said to Philippa. "I *know* you do."

She smiled at Carson. Then Philippa said, "And they lived happily ever after."

EPILOGUE

Carson Weatherell lived long enough to be able to cross the Atlantic in less than six hours. It was a trip, in fact, that she eventually needed to make with some frequency, if she wanted to see her grandchild and great-grandchildren.

During the summer after the one they spent in Portugal, she and Alec were married in the Old Bailey, and the following spring Carson gave birth to a boy, whom they named Philip, after Philippa. The following years were difficult ones to be living in London, and there were times Carson seriously questioned the wisdom of staying in England rather than removing herself and her son to Connecticut for the duration. But that, she always sensed, would have somehow felt like a betrayal. Not that she put herself or her son in harm's way; her contribution to the war effort was to manage one of the offices that helped find temporary homes for British children in the countryside, where they would be safe from the bombing that tore across England. Still, here in England was where the fight was—here was where the truth was, the heart of the matter that she'd first encountered during that summer in Sintra—and she could no sooner run from it than she could have stopped herself from taking a train to Cambridge on the off chance that one of Alec's friends knew something about a book and a ring. In fact, it often seemed to Carson that the lesson of survival she had absorbed in the summer of 1936—of setting one foot in front of the other without knowing what her ultimate destination might be, but trusting herself to reach it nonetheless—was the same lesson everyone around her suddenly seemed to need to learn quickly, once the sirens began wailing over the blacked-out city streets and the bombs began raining on row houses and palaces alike, and a kind of madness descended on London like a black fog that wouldn't lift.

For his part, Alec was recruited by Lawrence to join Naval Intelligence, where he did in fact use his skills at telegraphy and cryptography to become part of one of the most respected teams of code breakers in Britain. That team, thanks to Alec's own recruitment efforts, also included Thomas Brandon and Michael Morling.

And what of Freddy Hunt? Indeed: What *of* Freddy Hunt? It was a question that always remained with Carson. When Freddy disappeared that October day in 1936 down a twisting street in Cambridge, it was as if he'd vanished from the face of the earth. But he hadn't, Carson always suspected. Of course, it was possible that he'd hopped a ship, slipped overboard during typically turbulent weather in the North Sea, and drowned. Or that once British authorities had learned his secret identity, his German contacts came to regard Freddy as "expendable," and expended him down a London sewer. But it was, Carson felt, far more likely that Freddy had made his way safely to Germany and did what he'd bragged he would: contributed his knowledge of radio communication and physics to the Nazi cause. Then, she imagined, he lived anonymously in defeat, bitterly but unrepentantly, to an old age. Lived on and on and on, just as Carson and Alec lived on and on and on.

When the war was over, Carson and Alec reunited in London; Mrs. Bertram had died in her sleep of a heart attack during the Blitz, and had left her house to them. The place had been damaged by a firebomb, but in time Alec and Carson managed to make it their own. Alec resumed teaching, now at University College, London, where Carson enrolled as a student, studying Romance languages and literature, with an emphasis on Portuguese poetry. She wrote her thesis on the tradition of *fado*, and later the thesis was published as a book.

Like most children, Philip grew up to believe he had two sets of grandparents, though both of his happened to be on his mother's side. When Carson and Alec eventually explained to him, on his sixteenth birthday, the somewhat unusual circumstances concerning his mother's family background, his response was, not untypically for a teenager in 1954, "Cool." Philip had inherited not so much his parents' academic leanings as their political sympathies. Having grown up hearing stories of his father's mistaken arrest before the war, he had decided he wanted to be a barrister, and he eventually became Queen's Counsel, representing the Crown in important cases.

The story of Alec's arrest, in fact, did pass down from generation to generation, just as Carson had said she hoped it might on the night of Alec's party at Claridge's. Philip and his wife, Susan, a painter, passed it on to their three children, and Carson always suspected that the decision of their eldest, Veronica, to enroll in the graduate program in political science at Columbia University was motivated at least in part by having grown up hearing stories of political intrigue in prewar Britain. Carson got to meet the twin girls that Veronica had with her husband, a Columbia economist, but they were too young to hear the story from Carson herself. Carson hoped Veronica would pass along the family legend, and even asked her if she would, but the fact was, as Carson shuttled back and forth across the Atlantic at the turn of the twenty-first century, she had to wonder just what young girls today would make of such a tale from an era that even to Carson was beginning to feel like ancient history.

It was on one such flight that Carson Breve died in the spring of 2004. Alec had passed away the previous winter, during flu season, and though no one expected Carson to make the trip across the ocean so soon, she said she wanted very much to go. As Carson often did on these flights, she had been looking out the window at the ocean far below and thinking of the waves she'd observed day after day after day during her several crossings in the summer and autumn of 1936. Six days, this trip used to take; now, six hours. The world of 2004 that the eighty-six-year-old Carson Breve navigated effortlessly would have been more than unwieldly to the innocent, eighteen-year-old maiden voyager Carson Weatherell. It would have been utterly unrecognizable. Yet as much as the world had changed, Carson always felt that in some fundamental respects it was still the same—not just the same as it was in 1936, but the same as it always was. And all she needed to do to know she was right was to ask herself this question: What of Freddy Hunt?

Where *was* he?

He was, Carson told herself, everywhere. Slightly stooped now with age, his suit somewhat ill-fitting after all these decades, but still there: he might be that man coming at you as you cross Fifth Avenue on a beautiful spring morning in Manhattan. Or he might be whistling a nondescript tune as he shops a couple of aisles over at the hardware store in your town. Or he might be sitting in the seat next to you on a plane. It had long ago stopped mattering to Carson whether Freddy Hunt himself had actually survived. What mattered was that the spirit of Freddy Hunt lived.

But—and this was the important part to Carson—so did something else: a thought that made the thought of all the Freddy Hunts in the world somehow manageable. It was what Carson always remembered when this happened—whenever she looked out a window of a plane and saw the ocean far below and felt herself transported to a distant, sinister decade. It was what Carson remembered now, on this plane, when she felt a vague thrumming under her rib cage; what she remembered as she reached for her wrist, pushed aside a bracelet with blue beads, and felt her fluttering pulse; what also survived: the memory of a young woman with her life ahead of her, in the arms of a man with his life ahead of him, the two of them falling in love with each other, now and forever, on a night train to Lisbon.